Mi Reina

Don't Be Afraid

Fran Maklary

PublishAmerica
Baltimore

First printing

ISBN: 1-4137-0827-7
PUBLISHED BY PUBLISHAMERICA, LLLP
www.publishamerica.com
Baltimore

Printed in the United States of America

Dedication

For my daughters' incredible patience and infinite support—*Brittany and Chelsie*—Sent to me from heaven.

The man who has endured much by my side and who has my love tucked in the smiles of his children—My husband *Bill*—Thank you for your encouragement and undying emotional support.

The Rojas family—*My mother, Frances and father, Matias, and siblings, Stella, Sally, Jenny, Alfred, and Albert*

The Maklary family—*Julius (Mac), Penny, Dusty, Timmy, Kitty, and Kim.*

For having her son and for the love shown to me—My Mother-in-law, *Pat.*

For the craft of friendship—*Pam and Charlie*

Legal support—*Terry*

To the town of *Bisbee*—to those who have walked the same paths as I have for more than a century, and who share the same love for the community—Thank you.

To all who have given me friendship and to those who have shown kindness and unbiased support, I thank you.

And last, but not least—I wish to remember every single pet I have owned. For their loyalty, friendship, and for the company they gave me, during the times I had to endure loneliness.

God Bless you all.

Acknowledgments

True Catholic Site: http://www.truecatholic.org, and the address of the papal site, http://www.truecatholic.org/pope

Chapter I

A population from the past has worn a path toward me. Who are these forebears? They are individuals who have experienced a death by trauma, and they are commoners, aristocrats, and children; a populace of souls who have lost their way or refuse to believe they are now deceased.

I consider myself a born-again Christian, who holds the Catholic faith close to her heart and soul. I believe in God, angels, and Heaven. I have strong faith in Him and what He holds for every living and departed soul. I believe in a forgiving God that does not want His children to suffer, and wants all to find their way home.

I have always been sensitive to energies that electrify through unidentified presences. I never feel alone throughout my days and nights. When I am unaccompanied, I always feel an eerie and invisible companionship with supernatural forces. That powerful presence makes me feel special, yet at times, very frightened. Why me? Why was I given the gift of supernatural sensitivity? I am still formulating an answer.

I have only the knowledge that Christ has given me the special honor of hearing and seeing those who are caught and lost in the middle between home and earth.

I live in my hometown of Bisbee, Arizona, a community that is as interesting as it is historic. The town's nickname is 'the queen of copper camps.' Bisbee evolved in 1880 and was a boomtown in its early years. It was one of the great mines of the West.

While Bisbee was one of the greatest copper mining centers, nearby Douglas was the 'smelter city,' which processed great quantities of ore from Bisbee as well as from Mexico.

I still reside in Bisbee, which is now a tourist attraction, pulling people from all parts of the world. The small town tells its intriguing stories of its heyday through the beautifully designed buildings and the charming streets that resemble cities in Europe.

You can almost hear the yesteryears when the streets were filled with miners, cowboys, and prostitutes during a time when the mining camp was a boomtown, and its people were taking advantage of the great success of the mines and using their hard earned wages for buying whiskey in the saloons and for buying sexual conquests in the many brothels that lined the infamous Brewery Gulch.

I was born in 1966 at the Copper Queen Hospital and I am the next-to-the-youngest child in the Rojas family. I have elder twin sisters, Stella and Sally, plus an older sister, Jenny, and an older brother named Alfred. My younger brother is named Albert. Stella is living her life with her husband Dan, and their sons in Amesbury, Mass. Our father, Matias, sometimes called, 'Chico' or Frank, lives in his hometown of Douglas, a 25-minute drive from here.

Dad moved back to Douglas when our mother, Frances Quen Rojas, died of liver cancer in 1992. Her paternal grandparents were immigrants from France, and her maternal grandparents were from Pecos, Tex., and were Mexican American and had some Yaqui heritage, on her mother's side. She was a beautiful woman, with fine facial features and a personality both energetic and endearing. I miss her.

Her parents met in Bisbee. My grandfather was a miner and she, a young widow with three older children. My grandfather died of colon cancer at the age of 32. My mother was 18 months old and never knew him.

My father, had parents who were both from Mexico. His brother and sisters were all first-generation Americans. They were all reared in Douglas and some of them still reside there. He also inherited Yaqui lineage from his father, and Apache blood from his mother. My parents were married for almost 37 years when my mother passed away.

I married William, "Bill" (or as his family members from North Carolina and Louisiana call him, "Billy") Feb. 4, 1989.

I would have never believed, when I met my husband and reached for his hand for the first time, that he would be the same man who would stay by my bedside during the birth of our daughter, Brittany. He would be the man who would stay with me through 23 hours of hard labor, with our daughter Chelsie. He would be the man who shed heavy tears in the doctor's office when I was diagnosed with thyroid cancer in 1997. He would be my support system when I had to endure three days of incredible pain and the temporary loss of my voice, after my thyroid gland and five tumors were surgically removed from my windpipe. And he would be the man who would hold my shaking body, when we stood in front of my mother's open casket at her funeral.

Bill has never been shocked by my claims of supernatural sensitivity, but always listens intently when I tell him of my many paranormal experiences.

As for our two daughters and their feelings about my gift, they have different perceptions. Brittany expresses fear and tells me that she does not want to see an entity and hopes she does not have the gift of sensitivity passed on to her. I have a strong intuition that she already has. Her little sister, Chelsie, is a different story. She is exceptionally close to God and seems to have a very spiritual sense of awareness of His presence. Keeping her closed-lipped about the subject.

I have come to the conclusion that in the spirit-world, word must have gotten around about me as "the little girl who wakes from her dreams and calls to the dead." I believe they come to me for simple company or as a living-spirit who can show them the way to peace.

As a 5-year-old, my experiences of childhood encompassed Santa Claus, the Easter Bunny, and waiting for the tooth fairy as I drifted off to sleep. Mine was a happy and content childhood, until the summer of 1971, when my innocence was fractured by a circumstance I cannot even yet explain.

It revolves around a situation that for some is unfathomable. My entire immediate family was suddenly exposed to the afterlife. We were relentlessly haunted by two entities that refused to leave our home, the home *they* used to inhabit.

My family was a strong-bonded unit that survived and was drawn closer by these experiences. This childhood time-span covers earliest recollection of awareness of an afterlife in an interlude when I lived through strange and hair-raising circumstances, which opened the door to my future as a supernatural sensitive.

I remember being a typical little girl, a fair-skinned chubby Hispanic child with dark-brown hair brushed into tight braids or ponytails that reached the middle of my back. I spent many hours alone, because my brothers and sisters were much older and had other interests. I could often be found playing in the yard with my then-pet dog, 'Buttons,' a white shaggy creature, that followed me everywhere.

Stella and Sally, my siblings, who are identical twins, and the eldest children in our family, were both great influences on me. Stella was thin and dark-skinned, with long, black straight hair. She resembled a Yaqui princess. Her twin, Sally, mirrored her beautiful features. The two seemed to always be involved with high school activities while mesmerized by teen idols such as Bobby Sherman and David Cassidy, popular in that time.

My other sister, Jenny, was a preteen tomboy, who was very shy and kept to herself. She had very curly hair that she usually kept in a loose ponytail, and she dressed mostly in pants and tee shirts. She was by herself most of the time, and didn't show interest in playing dolls with a certain baby sister.

Lastly, there was my tall, skinny big brother, who did find time to play with me. Alfred didn't mind having me hanging around with him and his neighborhood friends, as they played basketball or football in the nearby park. He was the sibling my mother appointed to walk me nearly two miles each morning to my kindergarten class, telling me to "shush," and stop crying as he wiped my tears, reassuring me that I would see our mom after school.

My memories of my mother place her in her middle-30s making tortillas by hand, as an exceptional housekeeper who served full course dinners, according to my father's work schedule. My father was a typical blue-collar man, a laborer in the local mines, who never missed a day of work. He was a responsible employee and a good provider for our huge family.

I remember the summer between first and second grades as a time of coming to terms with a gift that would resurface throughout my life. It is my psychic ability to interact with the living dead.

"Goodnight, Mommy,"

"Goodnight, Mi Reina (My Queen)," replied my mother, as she kissed the backs of my hands, something she and I did before parting for the night.

As I drifted into a slumber, I felt a spiral of lightness and tranquility. Peace. Then a strong and magnetic feeling tugged at my spiritual being. I woke up confused. Hours must have passed. I could see my sister Jenny in the darkness of the bedroom that we shared with our brother. She was fast asleep in her own bed. I could hear my brother Alfred, breathing in measured inhalations and exhalations.

Through the bedroom window, I watched the dim moonlight streaming in. An illumination surrounded the room and shown just slightly, creating a beautiful glow. I sat up to a slender figure at the side of my bed. At first I could only make out the image of a woman. I could see her hourglass figure, a soft and feminine body shape. Her appearance seemed like a mirage.

"Stella? Sally!" I called.

The figure moved from the side of my bed and stood behind a lampshade on a nearby nightstand. The vision did not exert any control or negative vibrations, nor did she try to scare me. I only felt curiosity.

"What is it?" I asked. Suddenly I felt wide-awake. I rubbed my eyes with my chubby little hands and began to size up the circumstances.

The visitor's thin hands clung to the lampshade. Her fingers were long and tapered. My little voice seemed to spark her curiosity, and as I continued to call out to her, her head moved from side to side, seeming as bewildered as I.

As I sat in the darkness of my room, watching her step backwards and stand between my sister's bed and mine, I could hear the wooden floors creak under her light footstep. I could hear her long skirt brushing against her legs and boots and suddenly I saw all of her, in the moonlight. She was the most beautiful thing I had ever seen.

Her hair was in a tight chignon held by a large comb. Her eyes were gentle and their expression pierced my soul. She had on a long-sleeved, laced white blouse, with the collar up to her neck, hiding every inch of her skin. She had a tiny waist and wore a long, faded and worn skirt reaching down to her laced-up ankle boots. She was lovely.

The being stood there staring at me in utter silence. I realized she was not one of my sisters. I lay back down, with my gaze still locked with hers. Then she took two steps back and placed her slender hands into a praying position. She bowed her head and penetrated the floor, gliding down and out of my sight.

Somehow I knew I had been blessed with a visit from someone who lived long ago. I knew at that moment, at that instant that I was different. I felt secure and comfortable about what had just happened. It was for me to see and not for my brother and sister who remained fast asleep just a few feet from me.

As I tried to fall back to sleep, I remembered another time *she* visited me. During a recent morning, I had been playing with my dolls below an old Arizona White Oak tree, growing at the side of our house. That day the same strange feeling came to me.

My sisters and brother were at school, my mother was inside cleaning house, and my father was at work. Again, I was by myself.

My dog Buttons lay beside me, sharing space on an old baby blanket, as I played the parts of a scene I created with my dolls, I sang words to one of my favorite songs…

"…mmm mmmm, on my shoulders…makes me happy…mmm mmmm on my shoulders…makes me sad…mmm mmmm…"

The leaves of the acorn tree were falling slowly around me, making a slip, slip, slip sound, as they brushed the ground. Suddenly, my arms and legs had small goose bumps, and the warm breeze turned to cold. As the temperature fell around me, I sensed someone behind me.

"Is it time to come in, Mama?" I asked as I turned around, thinking my mother was standing behind me. When I turned, I felt only a gentle whirlwind filled with tenderness and warmth, yet not a person in sight.

I turned back around to face my toys, uneasy. I stood up slowly...then felt as if I had to run to the safety of my mother. Before I had a chance to move, I felt a gentle pat on my head and detected the hint of an unfamiliar perfume. I was too frightened to move a single muscle, almost too scared to breathe. I was still facing the tree trunk with my eyes tightly shut. The magnitude of the presence seemed unbearable. My tiny heart pounded hard enough to hurt.

I opened my eyes and looked down at my dog standing at my side. He was looking up but behind me, waging his tail.

"Buttons, I'm scared. Run, Buttons, run!" I screamed.

I dare not turn back around, fearing I might see *it*. I ran as fast as I could to the other side of the house, breathing heavier and heavier. My heart pounded harder and harder. I could feel this presence following me. I was horrified! The scent of the strange perfume followed me. As I darted through the back door, I ran straight into my mother's backside as she stood in front of the washing machine, doing the family laundry.

"Watch it, honey, and slow down!" directed my mother. "What's wrong?"

The impact woke me from my traumatic state. I answered in a low, timid voice, "I don't know."

Maturity began to be in evidence in that little girl. An "old soul," some would say, a child who was feeling absorbed in another realm, and a girl who was being followed by lost souls.

As more and more *visitors* came to me, I became more and more attuned to them. I began to see blurs of various individuals at the corner of my eye as they passed me. I became accustomed to taking a second look every time I would catch a glimpse of one of *them*.

Of course as a small child, I was mainly petrified of the supernatural and the many experiences of my childhood.

As each new episode occurred, my eyes would bug-out, and fill with tears as my heart pounded at an enormous rate. I would close my eyes as tight as I could, keeping the phantoms out of sight. I learned to pray to God…for His protection.

"God, pleases make them go away! Make them leave me alone. Please, God." Continuing with *The Lord's Prayer,* over and over, and over, again, until the strong magnitude of emotions would calm to tranquility, 'til I felt at peace.

I was still trying to fall asleep and remembered another time during a brisk, fall morning, when I was walking to school by myself. I had to travel by foot each morning and afternoon, to and from Lincoln Elementary.

About five minutes into my walk, my senses filled with the same terrifying emotions. I felt someone walking behind me. I turned around, but no one was in sight. The same sense only grew, regardless its invisibility.

My heart began to pound faster at the pull of the imperceptible being. It gained momentum behind me, as my walk turned into a jog.

I did not consider for one moment, to turn around again. I began to pray to God as my eyes welled with terrified tears.

As I began to pass the neighborhood fire station, located almost a mile down the road from my house, the feelings seemed to fade. As I took more and more steps, I could feel the entity pulling further and further away from me.

My school was now in sight and I could see the American flag whipping in the cool morning wind. I began to feel relief. In a few moments, my friends would surround me. *It* would leave me alone then…suddenly, I felt *it* standing directly behind me! I froze in my tracks at the entrance of my school. I shut my eyes as tight as I could, then turned my entire body all the away around. I took a deep breath and opened my eyes to see who was there. A horrific noise swept my senses. Whisssssss…scraaaaaaaaw…

With the eerie sounds came a blizzard-like temperature that penetrated my body and soul! The gust of haunting wind swept up my long ponytails and whipped me back into a brick wall.

As I bounced off the wall, I stood, with my knees locked and my arms and fists at my sides. My meditation began. I took in long, hard breaths, calming myself and fighting whatever was disturbing my living peace. I prayed to God for strength as I went into a deeper state of concentration. I knew I was stronger then what was disrupting my childhood. I was a living spirit.

As quickly as the zephyr had risen, it was incapacitated. When I opened my eyes, I saw the morning rays shining down on the dew, on the blades of grass below my feet. I began to shed silent tears. I remember feeling as if a grown man pushed me. He felt as if he was filled with great anger. He was nothing like the last visitor…nothing like *her*.

Suddenly I could hear children playing in the schoolyard and realized I was at school. I wiped my tears with my mittens and fixed my coat, then walked through the entrance to the schoolyard, feeling drained and uneasy. I couldn't tell anyone what had just happened. My friends would just laugh and tease me. This was a secret I would keep to myself, always.

I finally fell asleep that night and dreamed I was in a small cabin made of logs. I smelled the smoke of burning leaves outside the open front room window.

In the dream state, I felt terrorizing helplessness. I began to look around the small room I was standing in, and saw a fireplace with a fire heating a black pot of boiling water. I could hear the psss, psss, noise of water spilling over. I could hear the tick-tock, tick-tock of a large wooden timepiece hanging above the fireplace. I felt the cool breeze coming through the open window, as my nightgown and hair blew in the gentle wind.

In the next room was a square-shaped table with a white crocheted tablecloth. There were four chairs. The centerpiece was a large carved music box that was open and playing a sweet and gentle tune. The sun was setting and the room transformed into yellow-orange. I began to smile. It felt just like home. I began to feel safe. I was home.

Suddenly, the dream scene shifted and I could hear a familiar voice. It was *She* —"No! No! I can't, it won't come out," screamed the young woman. "God, help me!"

"You must push, Annabelle! Push! Don't give up. The baby is almost out!"

An unfamiliar woman's voice was yelling. I pushed open the bedroom door and saw a young woman lying in bed in a plain, white nightgown. Her long hair was put back in one braid and was messy in the front. She looked up at me and then looked over to the strange woman at her side. The strange woman didn't seem to realize I was standing in the doorway and never acknowledged me.

I began to cry when I discovered the young woman's thighs were covered in blood. I covered my eyes in terror and became nauseated when the scent of the secretions filled the room.

Instantly in my dream, I was at a funeral. I could hear the agonizing groans and sobbing of strangers who were dressed in black and surrounding a gravesite. A feeling of heavy, fierce sadness filled my heart as I witnessed two wooden coffins being lowered into the deep hole. One was long and the other tiny. Suddenly I could feel my body pull backwards, the scene becoming smaller and smaller.

"Mama, Mama," I screamed as I awoke from my paralyzing vision.

"Mama, please…Mama!" I screamed uncontrollably in a cold sweat and held onto my favorite brown, one-eyed stuffed, teddy bear, as I lay whimpering alone in the darkness of my room.

That petrifying experience shook my thoughts and senses into a new state of consciousness. The nights and days that followed those first few experiences were etched into the intellectual and emotional psyche that formed the person I am today.

The female apparition who chose me to reveal herself to me was obviously not the only presence sharing my home. It was shared with a negative male who seemed filled with suffering and pure darkness. He somehow dominated Annabelle with his lies and frustrations. He kept them both there, lost in time and in a state of dementia. The struggle between them caused uneasy energies that I picked up on and became a part of and was subjected to.

I have good memories of living on Tombstone Canyon. The sweet shaking tremors of the Cotton Woods caused by the cool breezes of living in the mountains and since we lived high on a hill, at the top of the neighborhood, we could easily hear voices and everyday commotion from the neighborhood below. The windows of the house were always open and allowed refreshing air into all of the rooms. One ordinary afternoon, Mother called us in at dusk to sit down for dinner.

"Francine! Come inside, it's time to eat."

As I walked into the living room from the front door, I could smell the mouth-watering aroma of fried chicken, and hear the crackling and hissing sound of the oil cooking the tender meat inside the brown, crispy skin. As I ran to the family bathroom to wash my hands, I could hear my mother yelling out the back door for the others.

"Kiddos, it's time to eat! Come on, let's go!" she called.

I lathered my hands with bar soap, squishing the suds through my fingers, feeling as if something strange was going to unfold. It was the beginning of my ability to forecast pandemonium.

I turned off the water faucet and reached for a folded pink towel, from the second shelf positioned above the toilet.

All of the fixtures in the bathroom matched in a pale rose pink color. The bathroom window had an old book holding it open, and the white transparent curtains were pulled apart, fluttering in a light breeze.

I took a step and stood in front of the billowing material, letting it brush my face, giggling as it caressed me. The breeze suddenly stopped. I continued to dry my hands with the towel, feeling the soft terry cloth material through my tiny hands.

I put the towel in the wicker hamper and snapped the bathroom light off as I headed into the hall that ran past my parents' bedroom.

As I walked through the short hall that curved around into the dining room, I neared a door that led to a steep staircase to our attic. It was one large room that spread the entire width and length of the house. At both sides of the stairs the walls seemed cold to the touch. At the top of the staircase was a wall full of pasted up coloring book pages. In front of the artwork was a wobbly rail of thin, frail wooden poles held together by wire.

The attic floors were of untreated wood that had splintered in several spots. At the west side of that garret room, was a beautiful stained glass window. The colors were bright, deep blues, reds, and greens, arranged in long, diamond shapes. During certain times of the day, the sun shone straight into the dusty room, causing prisms on the floor and back wall. The reflections resembled jewels in a pirate's treasure box. Sometimes I would stand in the middle of the room with my eyes open and spin and spin in a circle watching the spectacle of colors chasing each other before me.

As I headed toward that appetizing fried chicken meal at the dinner table, a knock at the attic door stopped me in my tracks.

"Tap…tap…tap."

"Hello?" No reply.

As I began to take a step, "Tap…tap…tap."

"Alfred you're not scaring me. Ha, ha, it's not working!"

As I stood there waiting for an answer from my brother, the doorknob began to turn.

"I said, you are not scaring me, turkey!"

The knob was still turning from left to right, and then suddenly the knob began to jerk up and down, shaking violently. I looked into the dining room and saw my entire family, waiting for me at the table.

I turned back to the attic door and could hear the sound of heavy footsteps climbing the stairs. Just as I began to reach for the knob to see who was there, my mother called to me. "Come on, pumpkin, let's eat!"

I raced to my seat at the table, resolving not to say a word about what had just happened. I didn't think anyone would believe me, and being a small child, thought if I didn't tell, then maybe it didn't really happen. Instead I accepted a plate filled with mashed potatoes, gravy, salad, and a drumstick.

I stared at my food, listening to the bustle of my sisters' laughter, my brother munching on his chicken, and to my parents conversing in Spanish. Then I heard unfamiliar voices. Strange murmurs came from outside the dining room window near the table.

I turned toward the window at my right and looked past the apple tree near the house. No one was there.

I picked up my chicken leg and sank my teeth into the tender meat. My father helped himself to a spoon of homemade salsa in a yellow gravy bowl, and poured it over his chicken. Then, simultaneously we all jumped in our seats startled by a shattering noise in the side yard.

Clank, clank, clank, clank! Bang, clank, bang!

We all froze, as the strange racket continued.

"What the hell is that?" questioned my father, wide-eyed.

Our five dogs, penned in the backyard, began to howl and bark uncontrollably.

"Whoooooo...woooooo...yelp, yelp, yelp," screeched the canines.

"Chico, what is that?" asked my mother. As my family appeared to be in a state of shock, I felt the same bitter coldness I'd felt on the way to school that morning. The racket grew louder. The noise sounded as if cans were tied to each other as someone dragged them around the house. The mysterious cans were being dragged from the side yard, up the back steps that lead to the backyard, then to the area where my parents' cars were parked. The racket traveled right through the dogs' pen and back around to the front of the house.

Everyone at the dinner table was in a terrorized state. My sisters were acting hysterical as the family dogs cried simultaneously in the background. When I couldn't stand it anymore, I got off my chair and ran crying to my mother. I was trying to speak between sobs, "Why are they here? What do they want from us?"

"What do you mean 'them'? "What do you mean, Francine?"

As I wailed in panic, the sound of the cans began to fade. The dogs gradually stopped their howling and barking diminishing to small yelps of fright.

"Can't you feel them? They're still here!" I cried.

My entire family just stood there, staring at me in complete confusion. Suddenly a new uproar began. Directly above the dining room table, in the attic, we could hear slapping and thuds, of a brawl.

There were sounds of an adult body hitting the walls and the sound of a head hitting the floor.

"Mommmmy!" I screamed.

At the same exact moment, as she made the sign of the cross, my mother yelled out in Spanish, "Jesus, Maria, and José!"

My father immediately stood up from his chair and marched toward the attic door in the hall.

"Who's up there?" he demanded.

A reply was not heard from the attic, but the sounds of a wrestling match continued. "Answer me! Who in the hell is in my house?" bellowed my father in a loud, angry voice.

My mother was still holding me in her laps and rocking me as she now recited the prayer *Hail Mary*, in English, "Hail Mary, full of grace; the Lord is with thee; blessed art thou among women,… "

My sisters were now standing behind us with arms and hands intertwined. Alfred had bravely followed my father into the hall. By this point, the fear had caught all of us in complete desperation for an explanation for what was happening.

Even as a young child, I was tuned into the spirit activity occurring in the house, and was conscious of having a deeper picture of the situation than the others. This somehow felt very natural and didn't frighten me, until that moment when I heard the beating.

"He's hurting her. He's hurting her!" I screamed.

"What? Who are you talking about, Francine? What are you talking about?" My mother questioned me.

At the same time, my father cautiously opened the attic door. As soon as he was able to open it wide enough to peek it, the commotion brusquely ended.

Dad and Alfred exchanged puzzled glances and chose to walk up the steps. The stairs creaked each time they moved closer to the top.

I heard my father express disbelief. "There's no one up here. What is going on?"

My mother turned me around to face her and asked me again, "Who are you talking about? What is it?"

I mopped my tears and sobbed. "Mommy, he is always making

her cry. She doesn't mean to make him mad. She just wants to sleep, but he won't let her, he won't let her!"

"Honey, (My mother's nickname since childhood.) nobody is up there," my father called. " I don't know what is going on." When he was finally back at the table, she said:

"Chico, I think we should talk to the Father. I want him to bless this house."

He shrugged his shoulders and matched his facial expression to his body language and said, "Everyone and everything are okay now. Come on, let's finish dinner. No more crying."

We all took our seats and wiped all our tears and tried to finish our meal. The temperature went back to normal. The dogs were silent. And I felt better. It was over, for now.

Chapter II

The next morning my mother called Rev. Gilbert Padilla, the pastor at St. Patrick's from 1970 to 1976. Arrangements were made for her and the Father to meet. The situation was evidently getting stranger and stranger by the day, and she felt that support from our church would bring back the family's serenity.

The two energies were allegedly fighting a battle of unknown causes and seemed to be more at ease when our family was in turmoil. Lately, my parents were fighting almost every day, and my brothers and sisters were matching the same type of feuding. At those times, the spirits seemed to be at their most calm. After the episode at dinner, and the first blessing (The ritual of a priest sprinkling Holy Water on a person, meal, object, or place, while invoking the name of Jesus, usually while making the holy sign of the cross of Christ.) of our home, things seemed to get worse.

On a particular Saturday morning, my sister Jenny, bared witness to another paranormal incident, as she watched television. The morning sunshine was streaming through the window facing the TV set, causing a vivid reflection on the screen. She said she could see herself on the screen along with the show. Unexpectedly, she saw a light and flowing puff of steady, what looked like cigarette smoke, being produced out of the thin air, through the same reflection. She turned her head slowly, and completely around, to see whom or what the strange fog was coming from.

A strong tobacco odor followed the smoke and was growing stronger and stronger by the second. She said she just sat there, frozen in time and watched the exhalations of an invisible smoker, unable to yell out for help. As she sat there in a state of astonishment the puffs and smell of smoke eventually began to disintegrate with the same eeriness as they first appeared.

Strange episodes, such as those, were occurring on a regular basis now, and advertising it to our mother every time one happened, was getting a bit old.

Another incident of supernatural power happened to my other sister, Stella. She said, when she gathered her hairbrush, toiletries, and a big thirsty towel, to prepare for a shower, an uneasiness came over her. Upon entering the family bathroom, the temperature fell quite fast, and her heart began to thump a bit harder. As she put her bare foot into the tub, she became more frightened and after taking in a deep breath, pulled the shower curtain closed, and almost immediately felt the presence of an invisible guest standing beside her.

Her immediate response was to run, but she instead turned to the shower fixtures and proceeded to begin her shower. Unfortunately, the heavy presence of a dark and sinister energy was too much to ignore. She hurriedly shut the water off, whipped open the plastic curtain, and climbed out of the tub. Her fear was gaining more and momentum as she grabbed her bathrobe and ran out of the bathroom, to our mother.

My father also told all of us of one particular incident, filled with the same type of eerie capacity. He said he was in the kitchen making himself a sandwich, when he heard the annoying sound of a bouncing ball in the adjacent bedroom. He said he let it go for a while, before screaming, "Francine, stop it!"

The bouncing noise continued regardless of his firm direction. He said he slammed down the butter knife covered in mayonnaise, and headed for my bedroom to investigate. When he entered the bedroom, it was empty. There was no child in eyes view, but the continued noise of an invisible bouncing ball was still echoing through his ears…and through his mind and soul.

A typical night in the house was filled with unpredictable occurrences, and at bedtime, my parents powered all the night-lights, but to everyone's dismay, unexplained forces shut them off. The weird noises and electric surges caused by the invisible visitors caused a great deal of fright among the family, forcing us to a high degree of uneasiness. So I was scheduled to sleep with my sisters on designated nights, to ease my own fear as well as some of theirs.

One particular evening, as I slept with my sister Stella, whose room was in the very back of the house, an add-on constructed by our father a few years after he purchased the home. I awoke from a light slumber and turned away from the wall and faced my sister. She was fast asleep, silent in her dreams.

Earlier that day, her twin, Sally, was reading her latest copy of a teen magazine, when she said she heard someone washing dishes. As she often did, she asked our mother for a glass of water to be passed from the adjacent kitchen window.

"Mom, would you please give me a glass of water?" called Sally.

There was no response.

She still heard running water and the sound of dishes being put in the drying rack.

"Mom? Did you hear me? I'm thirsty, can I have water?"

Silence was the only reply.

When she peered into the kitchen, no person was in sight.

"Mom! Mom! Oh my God! Mom!" she hollered!

This added more to the already growing list of strange incidents and to the fear of the household.

As I lay in bed with my eyes open and my arms tightly wrapped around my teddy bear, Freddy, I reflected on the events of the day. I began to feel odd. Suddenly, a sweet and gentle female voice was coming from the direction of the bathroom, which was the next room over from where I was laying.

The singing got clearer and louder as moments passed with ease. She was singing unfamiliar words to a lullaby in another language, but the melody she kept was enchanting, and ironically familiar. It sounded like the music box in my dream…

My eyes became heavy as I let out a long and drawn yawn, as I stretched out my arms. I closed my eyes and fell instantly asleep.

After I fell into a deep state of rest, I opened my eyes in another dream. I was still in my room, but it looked completely different. All of the beds were gone and in their place was a small empty cradle.

The headboard was engraved with ivy vines and rosebuds. Crocheted blankets were neatly arranged in the empty crib, with a homemade-looking stuffed teddy bear, at the foot of the bed.

Then I heard the same voice, singing the same lullaby. I looked around for the woman, but the room was empty. The crib began to gently swing by itself, side to side. The singing stopped, and in its place, a sorrowful cry began. Now the identical voice was expressing a horrible and mournful sob. It started out soft and grew into a deafening and bellowing cry.

I covered my ears and screamed, "Stop it! Stop it! Please, stop!"

"Francine, wake up. I made pancakes."

I felt the hands of my mother gently shaking me from my slumber.

"Mommy!" I squealed, "My mommy!"

The morning light was always a relief, but tension continued to build in our home, especially when my father had to work the graveyard shift in the copper mines. The nights were almost unbearable. Lights would go off and on, strange noises and footsteps would intrude our peace. After trying to deal with the negative vibes of the house for quite a while, It was decided that we'd all go to our Nana's house for a short time, to finally get a good nights' sleep. We were all so exhausted and drained.

The next day after I had the dream of the horrible crying, we piled sleeping bags, pillows, and favorite stuffed toys into the family station wagon, and drove to our grandmother's home.

Romalda Martinez Quen, lived in Old Bisbee, up Brewery Gulch, in a one-bedroom house. She was my maternal grandmother and at the time was in her late sixties. She was very thin, and wore her long, gray hair in a loose bun, often clasped by matching tortoiseshell combs. She wore wire-framed glasses and always smelt of lavender. Nana only spoke Spanish. We had a time trying to communicate, but always somehow managed. I was not fluent in the language (true to this day) due to the fact that my parents did not encourage my siblings and myself to learn while growing up. They apparently had trouble learning English when first attending elementary school.

Nana went to St. Patrick's Catholic Church every Sunday, adorned in a black, transparent shawl, placed over her head. In her purse she kept a perfumed handkerchief with flowers embroidered on the edges. She always used the same handbag when my mother took her to the store.

My grandmother babysat us on different occasions and always slept over. She chose to bunk with me during those visits. When it was time to go to bed, she would put a glass of water on the night table by my bed and would automatically reach for her Rosary beads, carefully placed near the full glass of water. She would kiss me goodnight on my forehead, lie back and then begin to pray.

I never disturbed her meditation and listened quietly with my eyes closed. I never heard her say, "Amen," because I would always fall asleep before she finished.

Her house was at the top of approximately 35 steps, as most Bisbee homes nestled in the terraces of the Gulch are. I climbed the stairs and saw Nana through the front screen door. As I clung to my pillow and my teddy named Freddy, I saw her waving hello.

"Nana, Nana!" I called.

"Mi muchacha del beb, viene aqua," (My baby girl, come here.) answered my grandmother. I ran up to her and received a kiss and a hug.

"This is going to be fun, Nana!"

After dinner, the sky had lost its sunshine for the day, and designated sleeping areas were assigned. My mother and Nana would share her bed, and the children would sleep on the living room floor, leaving our father to claim the couch.

We all decided to get to bed early, and before all goodnights were given, light snores began. I wasn't as tired as the rest. I lay on my back, gazing out the living room window.

The night sky was filled with glistening stars and a glowing moon. I hadn't felt so much peace in weeks. I was a mere child, but knew what serenity was. My young life had been interrupted with forces that drained me of childhood innocence. I was becoming more and more insightful of the *other side*. My intuition was gaining more and more momentum as the days led into night.

I turned over onto my stomach and closed my eyes and rubbed Freddy's worn paw, then fell into an uninterrupted slumber.

My parents shared our stories of the haunting with relatives, and much to their disappointment, they were mocked. My then, 20-something cousins, Peggy and Freddy (my Uncle Chuy's children) were the biggest skeptics. Peggy, the family comedian, dared her father and brother to spend the night at our house. The two spending a weekend evening with us, answered her challenge.

My uncle slept on the sofa and my cousin settled for a sleeping bag on the floor. After all the occupants of the house were tucked into bed and the lights were off, energies stirred up in the house without delay. The initial wave of strange sounds alerted Freddy first.

"What was that?" asked the ex-Marine/Vietnam veteran.

"Shush, go to sleep," answered Uncle Chuy. "You're just scaring yourself."

Footsteps walked back and forth over their heads, in the attic. The same was heard up and down the attic steps, along with other odd noises, making it hard for them to fall asleep.

Uncle Chuy had enough. He got up from the couch, and began to pace in the darkness. Freddy pulled the sleeping bag over his head, deciding not to show himself.

The next morning I ran into the living room to greet our guests, but discovered an empty room. My mother said they had left in the middle of the night. "Big chickens!" she remarked. "At least they believe us now."

Other relatives and friends still refused to acknowledge our encounters. The idea of recording the noises was brought up. A tape recorder was set on the bar that divided the living room and dining room, near the floor heater. The bar was oak and had a canopy and two cabinets, with stained glass doors, with two heavy-duty wooden stools with armrests placed in front of the furniture.

Next morning, while still in their pajamas, my siblings ran to the taping machine and rewound the cassette to hear what had been recorded. By the time the tape was ready, the entire family was assembled around the bar. The tap of feet and fingernails and heavy sighs were heard before the play button was finally pushed. Several seconds passed with nothing but silence, then, a slow and heavy pattern of footsteps was recorded, ending with a deep sigh. Then the tape abruptly stopped. Someone or something had shut off the recorder.

We all looked at each other and said nothing. It was a hair-raising moment and within seconds, my mother was making her way toward the telephone to call the local priest back to our home.

When the cleric arrived that afternoon, the day was settling into dusk and I was playing on my swing set. When I saw him drive up the steep winding road, I stopped swinging and felt an instant peacefulness heading my way. My mother had tried to follow a regimen of going to church every Sunday, but we never made it regularly. Despite that, I was very attuned to Christ and those who served Him. I understood that a priest represented God.

As he parked, the tires of his compact car made a crunching noise as they ran over the gravel across the narrow road below and in front of our house.

The holy man stepped out of his vehicle and placed a stiff white object on the roof of the car. He was dressed in a long, black robe. Never acknowledging me, he grabbed the strange object and inserted it in-between his neck and the robe. It was his Roman collar. After a few adjustments, he closed the car door and began his walk up the steep hill. As he approached the first step of the staircase, he saw me on my swing, and stopped to catch his breath.

"Hello, young lady. How are you, this evening?"

"I'm okay. Thank you for asking, Father," I replied.

I kept my eyes peeled on the man who looked to be in his early forties. He had jet-black hair, and seemed to have a thin build hidden under the dark robe. He had brown eyes that seemed kind. I was glad he was here.

As he walked through the gate at the top of the cement staircase, he asked if my mother was home.

"She's home. I'll tell her you're here."

I jumped off the swing and ran past him and up the second flight of stairs that led to our front porch. As soon as my bare feet touched the splintered wooden floor of the terrace, I felt the sharp penetration of a splinter in the bottom of my right big toe.

"Oweeeee! Oweeeee!" I wailed as I jumped up and down.

Instantly, the front screen door whipped open and out came my mother. Her makeup was newly done and I could smell toothpaste on her breath.

"Francine, what is the matter with you? The Father is coming any minute."

"He's already here, Mommy," I answered, as I nodded my head towards the priest who was still standing in front of the gate.

"Oh, Father, I'm sorry. I didn't know you were here," said my mother.

"That's fine, the child was on her way to let you know. I am sorry for being a little late, I had something else to attend to," replied the priest.

I hopped over to the cement porch stoop, sat down and brought my injured foot up to view. I could see the head of the splinter and removed the small piece of wood with ease. As I rubbed the sore spot, I could hear my parents speak to the priest. I went inside and stood beside my mother as they recounted the bizarre episodes that had unfolded in the past few weeks.

"Please bless our house, Father. The whole house is filled with something strange. We can't sleep..."

As my mother spoke to the priest, I turned around to a familiar sound coming from the hallway. I didn't move, but I could hear *her*. She was humming in a low and tender voice. I looked at my mother to see if she heard the voice, but she didn't appear to. The invisible carrier of the humming seemed happy the holy man was here. *She* was pleased. I turned back to the conversation.

"...Yes, I can see why your family is stressed. I will proceed to bless this home with the sanction that every child must be present. Each child will individually walk around the house with me as I sprinkle Holy Water and bless every room. They must learn not to be afraid of what may be here," replied the priest.

My parents gathered the family and assembled in the living room. The Father walked himself in and out of each room. After he explored the home, my parents escorted him into the basement, an area I rarely entered.

It consisted of two adjoining rooms. The entrance was in front of a crab apple tree that gave an abundance of tiny green fruit, every season. The solid wood door was at the bottom of five cement steps and opened to a dirt floor. My father kept his tools here and used the room for extra storage.

Near the entrance was a wire strung across the corner, where he hung his old Air Force uniforms. Some were covered in plastic and others uncovered, free to collect dust.

The room was large, and always stank of mold and dust. To the left, was another doorway that led into a second area of the basement. This was the room that I particularly disliked.

The room had a cement floor with three of the walls sheet-rocked. Upon entering, a cold draft would hit you like a brick wall. A dusty lamp—with an umbrella-like shade, lined in a silky salmon-colored material with fringe—stood in a corner of the room. At the farthest wall from the entrance, stood an ancient-looking bed frame with head and footboards. It was sitting on a man-made step-up, in an indention of the wall. The antique piece of furniture was creepy looking. I never stayed too long in that room. It was too frightening and much too cold to play in.

The rest of us waited patiently in the living room while the adults remained below. The house seemed oddly calm. I wondered what was going to happen next. I could hear my mother's voice as she and the two men walked up the front porch steps. As the door opened, I felt a flow of nervousness. A strange tension was slowly building.

The priest directed us to gather around the floor furnace that was in-between the living and dining rooms. He explained how he felt uneasiness there. We did as he asked and organized a circle, held hands and bowed our heads.

The Father began a full mass, there in our living room. He prayed for the protection and release of any suppressed spirits there. He commanded for those lost to leave, now. He offered communion and my parents and older siblings took the host, along with a sip of Holy wine. A blessing followed the Mass with Holy Water sprinkled in each room. He then, just as he said, led each of us individually into all rooms of the home.

When it was my turn to walk with the holy man, I stayed closely at his side and said nothing. When we walked into the twins' bedroom, he stood over Sally's bed and prayed louder and longer then he did anywhere else. I was occasionally sprinkled with Holy Water, receiving it happily and felt an exceptional amount of love and peace.

The ritual was completed as the entire property was blessed, as was every person and pet. The priest said his goodbyes and told us not to be afraid and to trust in God, "He is always with you children, do not forget."

I watched his every move as he walked through the door, down the stairs, and into his car. As he began his engine, my eyes began to water.

"Don't leave, stay with me," I said out loud and very quietly, as I stood at the door watching him drive down the hill and out of my sight.

Chapter III

After the mass was held in our home things quieted down, but not for long. The next visitation came to my mother during an afternoon nap, marking the beginning of horrendous events that followed.

My parents' bedroom was at the front of the house, next to the living room. It was furnished with a queen-sized, four-poster bed with matching red cherry chest of drawers and dresser. The bed was against the north wall, and to the left were two large windows kept continuously open during that time of year.

She dozed facing the window and the welcome breeze, eyes closed, when a sudden drop in temperature caused her to shudder. Almost subconsciously, she wrapped herself with her arms and tried to get comfortable for her nap.

Unable to sleep, she opened her eyes to curtains being blown up and down by a strange breeze in the room. In turn she quickly closed her eyes, and made the Sign of The Cross and repeated the words of *The Lord's Prayer*.

Comforted by her faith, she again opened her eyes to the terrifying sight of a white, transparent, eyeless face. With its appearance, the temperature became nearly frigid and the room filled with a mournful cry.

In a state of shock, my mother could not move, but found the strength to murmur, "Jesus, Jesus, cast out this evil demon, please, in the name of Jesus!"

Tears ran down her cheeks, her body paralyzed in fear, as the haunting drone of her unwanted visitor filled the room. The moans of pain and suffering were expressed through the hoarse voice of a depressed spirit. Having complete faith in God and all of His Saints, mother's power as a living soul grew strength as each terrorizing second passed.

Suddenly the temperature began to rise, and the distressing verbalization faded into an eerie silence. Mother opened her eyes expecting to see the unforgettable face, but rather witnessed the curtains being whipped straight to the ceiling. Then they floated gently back into place.

"My Jesus, thank you!" she cried. "Jesus, protect my children from this evil demon. Please protect, us Lord,"

The bloodcurdling event persuaded my parents to make arrangements for another house blessing. Father Padilla was not available so the Diocese sent a substitute from Tucson.

The next day, the entire family was crowded into the living room waiting for the man who would hopefully rid our home of the supernatural activity.

We were expecting him to arrive at 3 p.m. By the time he got there at 3:30, our young nerves were really on edge. When the knock finally came, it nearly scared us to death and sent us to screaming, as children will do.

Amused, my father chided as he opened the door, "You silly kids, get a hold of yourselves."

My father then welcomed Rev. Thomas D. Rice, who would later serve as St. Patrick's pastor during the years of 1977 to 1981. He introduced himself as he shook my father's hand, simultaneously blessing him by moving his hand in a cross gesture.

Turning to his family, my father introduced his wife, then all of his children by name. Then, without warning, it seemed, all hell erupted in our attic.

In shock, the priest turned to my father and demanded, "What's that, who's upstairs?"

The horrific sounds of another brawl emanated from the attic, but something new had been added. It was the thud of a body being dragged up the attic steps, its head bumping each tread, punctuated by the ominous grunts of over-exertion.

Strangely more concerned than frightened, I tugged my mother's arm whispering, "Mommy, mommy,"

"Shhhhh," she replied, with her index finger over her mouth.

"She isn't waking up this time. She needs our help!" I continued. It was clear that I had a deeper grasp of this scenario.

My mother looked down at me and said nothing as the priest asked with urgency, "How do you get upstairs?"

My father proceeded to lead the priest in the direction of the attic steps with all of us children following, until the priest noticed and ordered us to stay put.

From our vantage point at the bottom of the stairs we could see the door was standing open. To our surprise, the fight in the attic that had always stopped when investigated continued.

Being concerned or only curious, I crept around my family huddled at the attic door, managing to get within inches of my mother without her realizing it. I watched as the priest made the Sign of The Cross before heading up the stairs, reading from his book of rites and rituals. As he climbed, my father and brother followed close behind.

When Father Rice stopped at the third step from the top, he turned to face the large attic room. I watched the blood drain from his face. Without taking his eyes off the room, he extended his left arm to stop my father and brother, crossed himself and began to pray even louder in formal prayer.

When he reached the top of the stairs and looked back, he looked as if he were going to faint. Seemingly mustering more courage, he turned back and took a few steps into the room. The fighting stopped.

Father Rice quickly turned to the stairs and hurriedly tried to exit. Suddenly, he flew towards us, as if being pushed from behind. I recall my father screaming, "Alfred, grab him!" He landed on my brother, violently slamming both of them into the wall.

My mother screamed and attempted to push us back into the living room. Before I was forced to turn away, my child's eyes explored the stairs for someone to blame for the priest's accident. I saw nothing.

After assuring my dad that he had not been hurt, Father Rice led them back into the living room.

I have never heard my house as silent when the priest, with face flushed, my father shaking, and my brother pale as milk, entered the room.

Glancing at my mother in disbelief, my father admitted, "Honey, this is bad."

Tears in her eyes, my mother stated simply, "I know, I saw." Then turning to the priest, she begged: "I can't take this any more, Father, help us."

Confidence shaken, father Rice announced in a quivering voice, "I am going to ask St. Patrick's Church to hold a special mass for the public in the honor of your family. The extra prayers will add protection for all of you. Upon Father Padilla's return, I will discuss what has just happened and the urgency of the situation. I am also going to recommend an exorcism. The bishop must give permission before the ritual will take place."

Recalling the original emotions I experienced during that part of my childhood, I don't remember being in absolute panic. My emotional state was more of being oblivion of what was actually taking place. I did not know at the time that I was to become a magnet for the dead, through out my entire life.

My aura would be a sparkling light seen by those who were lost on the other side. The light that is seen by the dead is the same energy that gets me through each day of my life. That inner-self is the same that is dedicated to God.

The memories of being a little girl include being surrounded by a circle of lost souls. My frequent experience with the spiritual realm may have to do a lot with my hometown. People who have passed through or live in Bisbee have often claimed to sense a huge source of energy in the area. The town's rich background of success during its booming years drowned out the moans of past citizens who had been forced to leave this life in a traumatic way. Most of those individuals were new to the area and came to Bisbee for financial security and happiness. Besides the miners who ventured here for decent wages and stability, another source of income were sought after here as well. The profession of prostitution was without mistake, a major component of the booming economy.

Women came to Bisbee with the same hopes of financial solidity. Saloons were bustling with great activity, and up and down the

Gulch, one could see whores dangling handkerchiefs from rooms above the bars. Rooms and rooms bustled with activities of paid-for-sex. With the harsh profession of prostitution, a trickle-down effect lent an air of profound sadness.

Because the miners paid money for services, they would treat the prostitutes as creatures without feelings, often physically abusing them. The hurting didn't stop behind the doors of the brothels but continued with the wives who were betrayed, and to the children of the miners, who wasted their wages on selfish pursuits. These actions caused suffering to the point where scenes of drunken brawls turned into brutal murders. Bisbee has a history of a 'Wild West' realism that left receivers such as I, with horrid impressions from the past.

I am often hit hard with callings from spirits who seem to be mourning terrible scenes from yesteryear. If you took a stroll up to the base of Mule Mountains, you'll see miners' shacks still standing after a century of elements and modern production. Those old homes represent a time of glory gone by and continue to tell the sad stories of mining accidents, betrayals, and brutal murders. I have stood in front of one particular house that is located closer to the road then the others, which are nestled at the base of the mountain. The house faces the road in a diagonal position and is surrounded by trees. It has a good-sized porch with wooden railing. From the roadside, you can see the front door and two windows on either side.

On several morning walks I have sensed the presences of a small child and her mother. They seem to be waiting for someone. They tell a story of having been there since the house was built and are waiting for someone's return. I have not entered or further investigated, but hold interest each time I pass.

What happened there? Did the man of the house fall to a terrible mining accident? Did he find himself in the middle of a fatal bar fight? Or did he succumb to some kind of mining illness, like so many others? The strength of love that extends from a family that has experienced some sort of suffering may be the actual link from this side to the other.

After a lifetime of remembering the incidents caused by the first entities that managed to communicate with me a child, I have now reached maturity with my ability and have communed with the paranormal occupying my childhood house.

During a recent cogitative connection with those first two entities, I was flashed to why *they* are still there, imprisoned. Somehow, my sense is that the unspeakable occurrence in our home happened like this:

Hans and Annabelle began on the East Coast. I don't know the exact location, but the city is now a metropolis. Annabelle was a second-generation French-American 'princess' who came from a family of tradition and wealth. Her parents dreamed for her to receive a degree in teaching. Annabelle was a bright and loving person who always tried to please everyone around her.

Soon after graduation and in between her first and second years of college, she met Hans, a first-generation German immigrant. I see him with a medium-to-large build, average height and very muscular. He was a hard worker (miner by trade), and a dominant male, later becoming abusive to Annabelle. The two met and almost immediately fell in love. Annabelle's parents did not approve of her newly developed relationship, and wanted her to continue her education without distraction.

Hans, was very possessive of Annabelle. He did not attend school as a young child, but could read and learned to speak in English as a teenager. He did not care much for school or higher education and earned his way through life with the grunt of hard work. Hans was against religion while Annabelle was a devoted Catholic. He heard about Bisbee in the Territory of Arizona, through the miner's circuit.

He and Annabelle were married secretly against the wishes of the bride's parents and made their way to Arizona without saying goodbye to family and friends. When they finally arrived the first thing they saw was the Mule Mountain range, and found a place in the same area to start their new lives together.

Hans and Annabelle lived out of their covered wagon before eventually building their two-room house. Hans began to work in the mines and when he worked his 12-to-16 hour shifts, Annabelle devoted herself to creating a suitable home. She became pregnant months after they settled. Hans had expressed one of his biggest dreams was to be a father. He wanted his home to be full of children. He wanted his house to ring with the sounds of laughter, since he came from a home full of hurt and resentment.

When he learned the news of Annabelle's pregnancy, he was ecstatic and celebrated his joy with whiskey. Something that Hans did inherit from his father was dependency to alcohol. His incredible urge for whiskey turned Hans from a loving husband into a resentful and abusive human being.

He often cursed Annabelle and would rape and beat her, keeping her as his possession. He was brutal and she never stood up to him. She loved him and kept the secret and confided in no one.

She often passed the day crying while he was at away from the home, managing to compose herself when he walked through the door.

Annabelle was losing weight and suffered through many fevers due to an unidentified illness. They didn't have the extra money to see the doctor. The young miner's wife miscarried her first child. When her husband was told about the horrible situation, he became furious and beat her. She stayed inside for three days, to hide the bruises and to try to cope with the pain.

Annabelle became pregnant again, and took this expectancy to full-term. She delivered a tiny baby girl, named Jocelyn. The couple was submerged in complete happiness. It now seemed as if their life as they planned, was finally unfolding.

Annabelle was a very good mother, who met all of her child's needs. The sweet baby was healthy and greatly resembled her father. The young mother put her infant into the cradle that Hans made, and placed her on her tummy, singing a lullaby while she rocked the crib. Soon the child fell asleep, as did Annabelle in the big wooden chair placed beside the cradle. When the mother awoke she discovered her newborn daughter was dead.

Hans blamed his wife for the child's death and after the baby's funeral, beat Annabelle in a rage of insanity. With his bare hands he killed his wife, then himself.

They are still there, trapped in a world of suffering, blame, and torment. Annabelle still loves her husband and is trapped by her own loyalty and the hope for a child of her own. Hans is in a state of denial. He doesn't believe he has passed and is going through the same mood swings of an abusive alcoholic. He still expresses rages of anger and remorse for the death of his baby girl.

The feeling of being trapped in the spiritual realm must compare to the feeling of being in the state of a light sleep. During the first stages of sleep, sounds sometimes cannot be distinguished from real and from dreaming ones. In the supernatural state of being, one might not be able to distinguish death from existence. The souls who have become oblivious to the trials of passing time are surprised and maybe feel as frightened as those who are living in the very place they may have died.

Why and how does a soul become lost while crossing over to the other side? I have always believed that when a person dies through illness, accident, or even murder, the time of crossing is subject to an incredible amount of raw energy. When a person dies in a traumatic way, the electric energies leave. Is that cluster of pure force a soul?

God gave us the gift of free will that is a living, thriving conscience that directs the soul to make decisions throughout its lifetime. Why not be able to make a conscious decision during the soul's travel from life to death?

Maybe at the point when the soul is exiting its body, it condenses into a ball of electrical energy, and because of the soul's conscious ability to make decisions; it chooses not to cross over into the other realm. During that moment between Heaven and earth, the living soul has the ability to stop time. Not the normal seconds and minutes of earthly clocks, but the time of memory that can be replayed over and over again. A person can be in such a state of shock during the experience of death, that the very will given through God, may cause one's own suffering as an eternally lost soul.

A murdered wife forced into a state of shock may be confused into the disbelief of her own death, and the disturbing horror of her own husband and lover taking her life, leading her to stay earthbound. Such an example is the young Annabelle. The man whom she betrayed her parents for, the man who took her virginity, and the man who was the father of her daughter, destroyed her.

Annabelle could not feel the enormous hands of her husband wrapped around her tiny neck, squeezing every ounce of life out of her, but could only see his mesmerizing blue-green eyes staring back at her. They were still as beautiful as the first time she saw them, during that early summer in her hometown at the community picnic.

She began to gasp for air but could still not feel the painful grip around her throat. All she could concentrate on was the memory of Hans as he was standing under a large tree, clutching a branch above his head with one hand. She saw the sunshine gleaming behind him and the warm and gentle breeze flowing through his shoulder-length hair, as he gently smiled at her, piercing her with the same eyes that were now filled with insanity.

Suddenly the horrific pain of suffocation caused Annabelle to collapse, then fade into darkness, then finally, pass to her death. As she drifted into the whirlwind of demise, her memories of her life came to light.

The days as a small child sitting with her dog Mylo and her mother in front of the fireplace giggling, memories of her adult life with her husband during lovemaking, and the sweet memory of her sweet baby girl Jocelyn, penetrated her soul!

"No. It is not my time. It is not my time," argued Annabelle. With a spitfire blast of energy, Annabelle stopped traveling to the other side. She floated in time and awoke hovering above her husband. Hans was holding her limp and lifeless body close to his chest, rocking back and forth.

"Hans. Hans? Don't cry. I'm here, I'm right here. Can't you see me?" screamed Annabelle, unheard by the crazed man below her.

Hans continued to hold his dead wife's body and finally realized what he had done, and arose from his knees and began to scream, holding his head tightly, spinning around in circles, screaming,

"Gott! (God) What have I done? Warum (why), warum? I have no wife, no Tochter (daughter)!"

He fell back to his knees holding the dead body that was once his bride.

"Annabelle, my Anna. Gott, Gott!" cried the murdering husband as he slowly traced his index finger from her forehead, nose, then mouth, to her heavily bruised throat. He paused and took a breath as beads of sweat rolled off his forehead onto the bosom of the limp body.

He continued touching the body in the same way. Her breasts, then her stomach, then suddenly, he snapped again as he quickly looked up at her scarred neck. His eyes now dark with rage.

"You! Sie wertlose Entschuldigung für eine Frau! (You are a worthless excuse for a woman!) Weibchen! (Bitch!) You killed my Baby mädchen! (baby girl)" roared Hans.

In his complete state of madness, he turned his body completely around to face the rifle placed in the corner of the room. His tone instantly changed from angry to apologetic.

"Oh, my sweet Anna, Ich bin traurig. (I am sorry)" He repeated his apology several times. "Ich bin traurig ..."

Hans reached for the rifle, cried to a God he believed had forsaken him, and begged for His forgiveness and placed the gun to his chest. He pulled the trigger, but he did not hear the blast. With eyes closed he remembered his wife, sitting naked on her knees on their bed. She was beautiful in the light of the fire, her eyes peering into his, as her long and wavy hair caressed her bare breasts, filling his senses with pure excitement.

The bullet pierced his chest cavity causing no pain for Hans as he continued his path of memories from his life.

The first time he held his infant child: "Yes, Baby mädchen, I am your papa," said the young father as he cradled the babe in his arms.

The bullet passed through his heart and became lodged in the wall behind him, splattering blood and flesh on Annabelle and the baby cradle nearby. As Hans fell to the ground, he could hear unfamiliar voices whispering loudly in his ears. The same anger that drove him to act out dementia was the same negativity that held him on this side of death.

He found himself in complete darkness and touched his eyes, assuring himself that they were open. Too afraid to take a step in any direction, Hans stood completely still. Then, he heard her. It was the voice of Annabelle.

"Hans..." moaned the tender voice of his wife.

As Hans turned his head toward the woman's voice, his surroundings lit up with a bright glowing light. He could now see a figure of a woman standing in front of him. As he tried to adjust to the new light and focus his gaze he heard Annabelle calling to him.

"Hans, come to me," sobbed the young woman.

As the figure of the woman came into Hans' focus, he realized it was indeed his Anna. But, instead of wrapping his arms around her, he became engulfed in the same madness that drove him to the very situation he was in. He began to yell obscenities and throw and wave his arms furiously into the air, blinded by the possibility of ever finding peace.

Now, poor Annabelle and Hans would re-live the same scenes of suffering played out before and during the couple's death, held in a constant state of spiritual confusion.

As decades pass and various families live in the same place where the couple lived out their sad scenario, a spark of reality shines through their screen of denial, allowing them to communicate with the living, from time to time.

On occasion, certain activities of the living may make a haunting soul remember a time during their own lives, causing a sort of reaction and forcing supernatural energy flow into our realm. At the instant death penetrates this realm, may be the moment when will and fate collide. When a life is abruptly ended, a person may find himself in a serious degree of confusion and denial, a formula to become earthbound, to become heavy and magnetized to this place we call life. A place where a floating soul may feel strength by reliving a scene from his/her life, over and over, until it awakes from the sad, depressing state of refutation from realty, keeping it in the shadow of death, forever.

Chapter IV

This chapter is one of the hardest for me to write and also the most bothersome for me to reflect upon. I've touched, briefly, on the role of the Catholic Church in trying to bring peace into our disturbed home environment. Now I'd like to share in-extent how that all happened, so that you'll have a better idea of the happenings I went through as an innocent child uncomprehending the full process of an exorcism. Somehow, small as I was, I knew that the angels in Heaven would fight an incredible battle against a supernatural negativity in order for things to ever get back to normal.

As a grown woman, my research regarding exorcism brings the realization of what tremendous factors surrounded that long ago events; how serious the circumstances were, and how extraordinarily blessed my family was. I also understand that Christ has passed on powerful defenses to us, to use against demons and other negative forces.

Part of my research of the ritual, involved an interview with St. Patrick's pastor, at the time, Rev. Stanley J. Nadolny. He was ordained into priesthood in May of 1968, and came to Bisbee in 1995.

Father Nadolny said since his arrival he has performed approximately 12 house blessings in Bisbee, (One of which was done in my home and will be described in full detail later.) but denies ever witnessing an exorcism during his service here.

The priest explained that the Bishop from the diocese must give permission for an exorcism to take place. There are appointed Exorcists to perform the solemn rituals called "major exorcism or simple exorcism," to drive out evil spirits in the name of the Church.

Father Padilla sanctified our hearts when he blessed the home, but the entities probably hid and did not feel or hear him. During the second minor exorcism done by Father Rice, the unrested souls became agitated to the height of violence (pushing the priest down the stairs of the attic).

These holy blessings were probably the first callings of God that the lost souls had heard or felt in decades. The two entities probably blocked God from their existence in their deaths, and were now being summoned by God Himself. Spirits respond to successful exorcism with counter assault, as they try to stop the process. The reply to the ritual can be a stream of wild screaming and violence, all a collection of raw energy.

Father Nadonly explained that spirits do not possess homes or objects, because they have no souls. Exorcism is meant to drive out demons or dark spirits from the bodies and souls of the living, and has a lingering outcome on houses or sites where paranormal sightings have occurred. Persons who live in these peculiar places are pretentious to the vile actions played out by those who were there before.

This describes the situation of Hans and Annabelle. Hans had 'practiced vile actions,' and needed to be exorcised from this place of the living and with that, Annabelle could be released.

Father Nadolny said a major exorcism is for the express purpose of exorcizing diabolical spirits from the body of man. Although our house was not demonically possessed, the Exorcist, who entered our home may have read a simple exorcism prayer, to free our family from the entities.

Father Nadolny has not been trained to be an Exorcist, but gave the probability of the following steps before an exorcism will take place: an investigation to determine reliability of an alleged care of possession (haunting); committed of external phenomena; the witness (priest) must personally witness the occurrences of any activity; then determine whether that activity was caused by natural or supernatural agencies. Our house met those determinations.

Taken from the True Catholic Website: *The Holy Father exhorts priests to say this prayer (A Simple Exorcism) as often as possible to curb the power of the devil and prevent him from doing harm. It is recommended whenever action of the devil is suspected, causing malice in men, violent temptations and even storms and various calamities.*

We have the power given by God to fend against what is evil, as the church official did as he walked through our front door, that summer day.

Nervousness was by then a permanent state of being in the Rojas residence. From the harrowing gestures of my father, to the distressing howls and whimpers from our family pets, we were all at nerves-end. The over told stories of the haunting made us feel exhausted. We were anticipating the exorcism, living minute to minute.

I remember being told the entire St. Patrick's congregation was surrounding us with prayers. I don't know if everyone believed our stories of terrorism, by something supernatural, but members of my family felt their prayers, regardless.

As I sat down to a bowl of cereal, and a glass of orange juice, my parents began to discuss the 10:00 a.m. appointment with the official.

It was a perfect sunny, Saturday morning. The sky was a beautiful shade of blue with no clouds in sight. I could hear the pigeons cooing outside the window as I ate my breakfast. Morning breezes flowed through the front screen door. I closed my eyes and breathed in the cool air. Today was going to be the beginning of something I hadn't felt in months, quietude.

"Francine, hurry and finish. You need to get dressed and make your bed. Clean your room, too. The Father will be here later this morning."

I looked at my mother as she took my empty bowl and glass, and wondered if she was scared. She never asked me about the woman I told her I had seen, or how I knew *he* was hurting *her*, or about the strange singing I heard.

"Mommy, will the bad man go away when the Father comes today?" I asked.

My mother stopped clearing the breakfast table and sat across from me.

"Mi Reina, don't be afraid. Whatever has been making us crazy these past months will be faced with the power of God today," said my mother, holding my two hands close to her heart.

"Do you promise, mommy?"

"I will say this to you. I believe in God and trust Him from top to bottom. He loves you, me, your brother and sisters, and your Dad. Trust God," declared my mother.

I stood up and walked toward her and wrapped my little arms around her. I touched her cheek and tapped her nose. "I love God, like I love you. I will be good, Mommy," I said as she simultaneously kissed my forehead.

"Things will be better today, you'll see. Now go and get dressed, so I can clean up."

The rest of the morning seemed to fly by and was unusually quiet. I was sitting on the back steps brushing Buttons when I heard my parents welcome the official into our house.

My brother, Alfred, came to the backdoor screen and informed me, "Mom said it was time to come in."

I stayed with Buttons for a few more minutes before I went inside. I was apprehensive for what might happen next, and what might not happen at all.

The ritual began almost immediately after the holy man arrived. We all gathered in the living room and watched the Exorcist who was dressed in the traditional long, black Cossack, and Stole (A reversible, short scarf worn around the Exorcists neck.) as he began to set up for a full mass.

The Mass began with a sermon about the grace of God and the unrested souls inhabiting the house, I began to hear *her.* She was humming the same lullaby and seemed to recognize a religious service. She radiated pleased feelings to me. I looked around the room to see if anyone else noticed the low humming, nobody seemed to.

The officiant was positioned near the floor heater that had earlier been tagged as some sort of vortex. During the Mass, my parents were standing side by side in the front, my sisters stood in a second row, and Alfred and I were in the back. At the end of the Mass, everyone but I received Communion. At the time I had not yet taken the sacrament of my first Communion, but I was blessed with sacred oil on my forehead. The Priest said he would now begin the exorcism.

"I will recite the words of the ritual and walk through each room of the house as I bless each corner with holy water. Please, all of you, follow closely behind, and fear nothing, for Christ is here," said the church representative.

We assembled in the same formation that was used in the living room, with the exception of mine. I was pushed up to the front to stand between my parents.

The Exorcists was holding a book with rites and rituals of the Catholic Church open, with a crucifix laying flat in its crease. He began to whip holy water from his silver scepter, and started to read the following aloud in Latin

This prayer was taken from the True Catholic Website: *"This is the Prayer to St. Michael the Archangel: In the name of the Father, and of the Son, and of the Holy Ghost. Amen..."*

We were still in the living room. The house was still seemed calm, and I couldn't hear *her* anymore.

"...Most glorious Prince of the Heavenly Armies, Saint Michael the Archangel, defend us in "Our battle against principalities and powers, against the rulers of this world of darkness, against the spirits of wickedness in the high places." (EPH.,6,12) Come to the assistance of men whom God has created to His likeness and whom He has redeemed at a great price from the Tyranny of the devil. Holy Church venerates thee as her guardian and protector; to thee, the Lord has entrusted the souls of the redeemed to be led into heaven..."

We paused at the entrance between the dinning room and the kitchen. Then, he shook his scepter three times around the kitchen and continued.

"...Pray therefore God of Peace to crush Satan beneath our feet,

that he may no longer retain men captive and do injury to the Church. Offer our prayers to the Most High that without delay they may draw His mercy down upon us; take a hold of "the dragon, the old serpent, which is the devil and Satan, "bind him and cast him into the bottomless pit..." that he may no longer seduce the nations."(APOC. 20, 2-3)..."

Suddenly, as we walked through the kitchen a slamming door echoed throughout the house. We all stopped in our tracks. The father paused, and continued reciting as he walked into my bedroom.

"...Exorcism: ...In the Name of Jesus Christ, our God and Lord, strengthened by the intercession of the Immaculate Virgin Mary, Mother of God, of Blessed Michael and the Archangel of the Blessed Apostles Peter and Paul and the Saints (and powerful in the Holy authority of our Ministry), we confidently undertake to repulse the attacks and deceits of the devil..."

As I followed along, I felt a tension building. The house seemed to tremble, like a scared animal. I could hear the sound of a howling wind beginning to build. I held on tightly to the hands of both parents.

"...Psalm 67: ...God Arises: His enemies are scattered and those who hate Him flee before Him. As smoke is driven away, so are they driven; as wax melts before the fire, so the wicked perish at the presence of God. (Verse cal) Behold the Cross of the Lord, flee bands of enemies. (Response) The Lion of the tribe of Juda, the off spring of David, hath conquered. (Verse cal) May Thy mercy, Lord, descend upon us. (Response) As great our hope is Thee..."

We had traveled through the bathroom and continued to follow the Exorcist as he proceeded to sprinkle holy water in every room. As we neared the hallway of my parents' room and attic entrance, the Bishop paused once more and continued the ritual in a louder voice.

"... We drive you from us, whoever you may be, unclean spirits, all satanic powers, all infernal invaders, all wicked legions, assemblies and sects. In the Name and by the power of Our Lord Jesus Christ, (here, a blessing with a crossing motion was made by the official) *may you be snatched away and driven from the Church of God and from the souls made to the image and likeness of God and redeemed*

by the Precious Blood of the Divine Lamb. (Another blessing motion made)... "

The windows in my mother's bedroom began to quietly rumble and vibrate, then suddenly quake!

One of my sisters screeched in fear, but the priest chose to ignore the scene and headed for the attic door. As he opened the door, he interrupted his narration by blessing the staircase in a much more aggressive way than he had before. He turned and faced us while motioning not to follow and climbed the stairs alone. We stayed silent and listened for his voice as he quoted from the book of rituals.

"*...Most cunning serpent, you shall no more dare to deceive the human race, persecute the Church, torment God's elect and sift them as wheat.* (Crossing motion) *The Most High God commands you,* (Crossing motion) *He with whom, in your great insolence, you still claim to be equal. "God who wants all men to be saved and to come to the knowledge of the truth" (I Tim. 2,4)...*

I looked up and watched the thin rail at the top of the steps start to shake, then right before my eyes, the stairway walls began to wave in and out, like ripples of water. A low deep murmur began to flow from the walls of the attic above us. We were in a frozen state of shock and didn't move.

The Bishop was now in full view with his face seeming stern and eyebrows clenched closely together, yet maintaining his composure. His pace was slow and steady as he descended the stairs.

I was freezing and realized my teeth were shuttering uncontrollably. I looked up at my mother and could see her breaths in the frigid air. My heart was beating hard enough for me to hear.

As the Exorcist neared the last step, we backed up and made way for him to walk through. He closed the door, and behind it we could literally hear screams of torment. By now, my sisters were in tears and I also began to feel my own tears run down my face. Not only was I terrified by the whole experience, but I could also feel a tremendous amount of sadness surrounding me.

The Holy Man led us through the dining room and stopped dead in his tracks as the laundry room door whipped open and slammed shut!

In my own ears, I heard the humming of intense winds whirling around the room and as I looked over to the priest, whose eyes were closed, as he continued to recite further into the prayer, had seemed to gain a Devine strength and was executing it through his voice, which seemed to come from the very bottom of his diaphragm.

*"...God the Father commands you. (*Crossing motion) *God the Son commands you.* (Repeat of crossing motion) *God the Holy Ghost commands you. (*Crossing motion) *Christ, God's Word made flesh, commands you; (*Crossing motion) *He who to save our race outdone through your envy, "humbled Himself, becoming obedient even unto death." (Phil. 2,8); He who has built His Church on the firm rock and declared that the gates of hell shall not prevail against Her, because He will dwell with Her. All days even to the end of the world." (Matt. 20, 28)...*

The holy man grabbed the doorknob of the swinging door and entered the small laundry room. By now the howl and whimpers of our canines were at full force. I could see the dogs pace back and forth through the utility room windows and could sense their confusion and fear.

"...The sacred Sign of the Cross commands you, (Crossing motion) *as does also the power of the mysteries of the Christian Faith.* (Crossing motion) *The glorious Mother of God, the Virgin Mary, commands you;* (Crossing motion) *she who by her humility and from the first moment of her Immaculate Conception crushed your proud head. The faith of the holy Apostles Peter and Paul, and of the other Apostles commands you. (*Crossing motion) *The blood of the Martyrs and pious intercession of all the Saints command you.* (Crossing motion) *Thus, cursed dragon, and you, diabolical legions, we adjure you by the living God,* (Crossing motion) *by the true God,* (Crossing motion) *by the holy God,* (Crossing motion) *by the God..."*

The door ceased its activity. We followed the priest outside and down the back stairs as we assembled in front of the basement door. He continued with the ritual.

"...Who so loved the world that He gave up His only Son, that every soul believing in Him might not perish but have life

everlasting" (St. John 3, 16); stop deceiving human creatures and pouring out to them the poison of eternal damnation; stop harming the Church and hindering her liberty. Begone, Satan, inventor and master of deceit, enemy of man's salvation. Give place to Christ in Whom you have found none of your works; give place to the One, Holy Catholic and Apostolic church acquired by Christ at the price of His Blood. Stoop beneath all-powerful Hand of God; tremble and flee when we invoke the Holy and terrible name of Jesus, this Name which causes hell to tremble, this Name to which the Virtues, Powers and Dominations of heaven are humble submissive,..."

The basement was freezing, the air almost too cold to breathe in. I didn't want to be in there! Something bad happened in there, I could feel it. The sounds of a woman crying deafened my ears and I covered them to try to block *her* out. Her voice echoed throughout the entire basement, sending gushes of blood toward my chest, hardening my body muscles as she took more breaths to complete her agony of terror.

We all walked into the most frightening room of the entire structure and huddled closely together.

Suddenly, the old bed frame started to shake, then gradually sway and drag from side to side, hitting the damaged wall every time. A man's voice roared nasty obscenities, then turned from a human tone to a deep and raspy, animalistic cry, as the exorcism continued.

"*...this Name which the Cherubim and Seraphim praise unceasingly repeating: Holy, Holy, Holy is the Lord, the God of Hosts. (Verse cal) O Lord, hear my prayer. (Response) And let my cry come unto Thee. (Verse cal) May the Lord be with thee. (Response) And with thy spirit. Let us pray: God of heaven, God of earth, God of Angels, God of Archangels, God of Patriarchs, God of Prophets, God of Apostles, God of Martyrs, God of Confessors, God of Virgins, ...*"

The holy officiate, was now yelling the words and spreading holy water in every corner of the room simultaneously. Suddenly the woman's voice came back sounding as if she were in a great deal of pain. The scene was awful! Just when I thought I couldn't take another second of it, the howls ceased.

"...God who has power to give life after death and rest after work: because there is no other God than Thee and there can be no other, for Thou art the Creator of all things visible and invisible, of Whose reign there shall be no end, we humbly prostrate ourselves before Thy glorious Majesty and we beseech Thee to deliver us by Thy power from all tyranny of the infernal..."

The bed stopped moving, the voices stopped, and the temperature began to rise. *"...spirits, from their snares, their lies and their furious wickedness. Deign, O Lord, to grant us Thy powerful protection and to keep us safe and sound. We beseech Thee through Jesus Christ Our Lord. Amen. (Verse cal) From the snares of the devil, (Response) Deliver us, O Lord. (Verse cal) That Thy Church may serve Thee in peace and liberty: (Response) We Beseech Thee to hear us. (Verse cal) That Thou may crush down all enemies of Thy Church: (Response) We beseech Thee to hear us..."*

The last of the exorcism prayer was recited in the living room. The entire process lasted a bit longer then anticipated and seemed to drain all of us to pure exhaustion. The church official said he felt a greater amount of peace in the house and hoped the exorcism was a success. He left our home seeming also weakened by the experience.

As he said his goodbyes, he blessed all of us with his hand in a crossing motion and before walking through the front door, bent down to me and said: "A child as small as you must have the strength of a warrior angel. Bless you," while patting me on the head.

I gave him a slight smile and nodded in agreement.

That day was a remarkable glimpse into the pure power of Christ. He is the sole leader of this universe and brought fury to the entities that were disturbing faithful, living souls, and shot a nice dose of reality into *them.*

After the purification of our house was done, the strange noises and phantasmal visions stopped. The question is if the supernatural events ceased completely in that house? I don't know, but I hoped as a young child, the woman I had seen would finally be able to rest and prayed the male presence would ultimately leave her alone and also find peace.

My childhood was given back and seemed to be normal again. I was finally able to dream sweet scenes filled with cotton candy and pudgy puppies. My soul was now undisturbed and I too, was at peace, for the moment…

Chapter V

The years rolled by and my connection with the supernatural world intensified as wildly as my adolescent emotions did.

My family experienced many changes during my preteen years, including moving from Hans and Annabelle's house and into a much smaller residence, closer to Bisbee's Main Street and to Brewery Gulch.

The mines closed a few years earlier due to several business reasons and along with the rest of the kinship of the Phelps Dodge Company; hard times were hovering above all. Because of the closure, my father was out of work and we were out of money.

The results of sharing a tiny three bedroom house with seven other people and living in a densely populated neighborhood was enough to deal with, but messages from the departed that were being received, was just another thing to contend with.

During many evening hours a piercing fear seemed to be with me as I slept. Slow, flowing, magnetic sensations pulled me from a deep slumber, as my bedroom would fill with the presence of many strange visitors, coming for answers and directions.

Many of my supernatural experiences I have encountered in Bisbee are closely tied to its history, which must be told in more detail to define the energies felt along Brewery Gulch, Main Street, and many other area residential sites in the old mining camp.

The complete devastation of the past existence of people that lived mostly in pure sin was sometimes too hard for a mere child as myself to withstand. I was in a state of unholy terror as my own living soul was being pierced by the red-evils of Bisbee's bizarre and renegade past.

I was picking up on the energies of those irreligious, greedy citizens of Brewery Gulch, celebrating their free time with blind pleasures and even still, after their death, trying to find their place.

The high wages given to the Copper Queen miner attracted a variety of people to the very rough, but beautiful Mule Mountains and to Brewery Gulch, an area located at the intersection of Mule Gulch, now called Tombstone Canyon.

Brewery Gulch's population was building so much momentum, from it's raw and wild reputation of gambling, saloons, and prostitutes, that this one-liner, "The hottest spot between El Paso and San Francisco," has become one of the most describing said about the rowdy neighborhood of its time, and commonly used today by local businesses advertising the area.

The Gulch became an incredible canvas of alcoholic businesses that went instantaneously up, as soon as news of the mining camp rang through the territory, with great success and speed. Of course one might suspect thriving drinking establishments would bring in prostitutes and gambling, a true assumption.

Many types of people trekked in and out of Bisbee, including young and innocent adults trying to survive however they could, using whatever they had, including their own bodies. Those prostitutes held a big part of Bisbee's most infamous neighborhood's history, which became a very organized form of business that was mostly brought to its succession in the higher part of the neighborhood, called Zacatecas.

Historians claim that 'row houses' or 'cribs' were established in that same vicinity. These sinful quarters were said to have been very long in dimension and divided into several rooms, with individual entrances leading to the street.

Incredibly, the cement foundation of the buildings still exist with weed-filled lots, and at certain times of the year, full of tumbleweeds along with bad impressions of sadness and suffering from the 'services' played out in scenes of strange and self-inducing activity.

After a short time of news of almost certain success in Brewery Gulch was spread, gambling played a grand part in the small watering holes eventually becoming ostentatious establishments for the community. With the change of 'higher class' of clientele in the

Gulch, came greater amounts of monies spent, pulling in more and more people into the wild neighborhood, and town of Bisbee.

Politicians and executives were not the only people spending 'big money' up and down the Gulch, but local miners were also known to spend a 'bundle.' My mother told me of how my own grandmother and her friends despised the nasty saloons that ravished their own family wealth, from time to time. She said the bars never closed, they stayed open from morning to night, to night to morning.

Eventually, prostitutes were not allowed in the saloons of Brewery Gulch and were forced to work in the designated 'red-light district.' The woman of the Gulch were probably treated well, but from time to time, unthinkably abused. So many stories have been told by generations of Bisbee Natives regarding treatment of these females, generating from beatings, stabbings, and horrible attacks of gang raping.

The prostitutes must have felt alienated from family and friends. Most would have traveled from afar, alone and sadly very young. The miners of the time were considered rough-types, cheapskates, and cheaters, and for a woman of the night to have to deal with the horrors of such a life, ancestors tell stories of their drug addiction, and incredible alcoholic abuse.

Even though there was the rule of no whores in the saloons, the prostitutes stubbornly ignored the ordinance and worked out of the rooms located extremely near the many hidden stairways in Brewery Gulch. Here was a spot where rowdy men and women did unspeakable deeds, where psychic impressions were made and where my supernatural experiences continue.

The lost souls of the Gulch are attracted to present individuals with strong beacons of light that could lead them back to a vile and indecent time of Bisbee's past. These females, sad and violated from their own innocence, seem to still hold claim to Bisbee and make their presence known.

As a young girl in the late seventies, Brewery Gulch was a lot more suitable for families to live in. The same saloons were still there, but now called bars, and gambling and a red-light district no longer legal.

By the end of the school day, I would forget the uneasy time of night by enjoying the sunlight of the afternoon during the bus ride home after a full day of sixth grade.

I would step off the school bus at the Lyric Theater stop, and begin my walk home though several shortcuts. Instead of walking through the Gulch to get home, (I was not allowed to walk past St. Elmo's Bar situated in the middle of the street. I had to literally walk around the neighborhood.) I would walk through the Copper Queen Hotel's plaza, back to the pool, and out the back gate. Beyond the Hotel's fence is an alley leading up to a set of stairs that finished with the road to my house. In-between the hotel and the staircase are another set of stairs, named "Broadway Steps," that lead down into Brewery Gulch.

As I walked through my shortcuts, I often had the urge to turn around and see who was coming up on me. But every time I looked back, I saw no one and continued on. I would explore the lower half of Tombstone Canyon with every spare moment I had. During one exploration, I came upon something I did not expect.

When I arrived home from a late Saturday matinee, at the Lyric Theater, I interrupted a private conversation between my mother and her friend. My mother asked me to go outside, she said she needed the privacy.

I decided to take a walk. As I left my front porch, I noticed the desert sky turning to the glow of orange, purple, and sorbet pink, the colors of low, but energizing cosmic energy.

I headed toward the place where I found complacency and away from any kind of tension. That sweet place was the stairway that led down from the upper part of the neighborhood toward Brewery Gulch. The stairs are ancient and produce an incredible amount of vitality from its exciting past, plagued with energies from those who have traveled its path.

As I made my journey toward my spot, I began to take in the sweet smells of the huckleberry vines growing on most of the chain-linked fences of small houses that lined Taylor Avenue. To get to my destination, I had to take another set of cement steps that were steep and directly of the left side of Central School. (The building is the site of the first one-room school house in Bisbee.)

As I descended the stairs, my stomach tightened and my fingers began to tingle. As soon as I caught the first glimpse of my favorite spot, I began to jog toward it. When I got to the top of the staircase, I stood on the first step for a few seconds before stepping down more. The sun was still shining down through the thick branches of trees and pomegranate bushes lining the sides of the stairway, causing the cement to glimmer and shine.

As I strolled down the stairs, I began to smile and feel rejuvenated after feeling alienated from my own home. I happily tugged at the leaves brushing my head and found a spot to sit down. I closed my eyes and began to meditate.

Almost immediately, I felt a breeze stir around me. The dead leaves scattered on the surrounding ground began to slide and hop toward each other, making scratching sounds on the concrete. The dry material gained momentum in the gentle wind. As the breeze took strength, I opened my eyes to the small cyclone of leaves twirling in midair.

Just then, the essence of a light perfume became evident and intensified as each motion of the spiral of dead leaves took speed.

I wasn't frightened at first, but my senses were filled with the energy of several presences. They were of young women whose voices began to whisper. I couldn't understand their words, but could hear all of the different tones of voices.

"Who's there? What do you want?" I said out loud as I gripped the edge of the cold cement.

The sound of soft whispers grew to an ear cracking volume accompanied with numerous pairs of feet shuffling around the stairs, positioning themselves completely around me. The entities executed depressed emotions bringing me to tears.

"...shhh...shhh...shhh," murmured the invisible company.

I suddenly had the urge to close my eyes in response to a warm and a high-powered breeze that penetrated my entire body. As I took a long soft breath, my mind was shocked as vivid pictures of each entity were etched into my thoughts and soul:

Bianca…a small and fair-skinned Mexican, wearing an off white, underwear looking, linen material, with a tight bodice covering her tiny waist; Gretchen…a chubby blonde who appeared to be middle-aged and wrinkled, and Alana…she was beautiful. Her long, dark and wavy hair was pulled back with oversized, silver hair-combs…

In an astonishing moment, a feeling of holy terror rang through my bones! Screeches of blood curling screams forced me to cover my ears as jolts of a pain shot through them.

The echo of shrieks from the female apparitions suppressed extreme anxiety slinging the spirits together into one large white cluster of fog that zipped quickly up to the top of the stairs, with the poignant screams following closely behind. The ball of mist sifted to the left of the stairway and disappeared, leaving a haunting silence in its place.

As I let out a loud shriek, I covered my eyes to what sounded like a group of footsteps ascending the cement steps below me. The stairway curved as it crawled up to my feet, as did the sounds of a rowdy group of men climbing closer and closer. I could hear the deep tones of laughter of several people and the clinking of their bottles quickly nearing.

As I took a few small side steps to the vines growing on the fence on the right, another chilling gust of wind was present. I could see my breath as the spine-chilling air surrounded my petite body.

The men's voices were upon me in an instant. I couldn't see the invisible phantoms but could smell liquor and vomit filling the air. I became nauseated and responded to the frightful scene with instant gagging.

The scene seemed to play out in a jerky slow motion. The dark energies were going through me in a slow and shaky motion. The saturation of evil was almost painful.

I was able to bring my young spirit to strength and automatically began to pray out loud, whipping the tears from my eyes with the left hand, while the right made the sign-of-the-cross.

"God…"

"Hail Mary, full of grace; the Lord is with thee; blessed art thou among women, and blessed is the fruit of thy womb, Jesus. Holy Mary Mother of God, pray for us sinners, now and at the hour of our death. Amen."

It didn't take long before the light of God and his angels overpowered the moment with heavenly peace. My plea was answered.

The cold spirits dissipated from my space and moved into an abandoned house positioned on the left side of the stairway, across from where I stood and where the female banshees seemed to travel too.

The celebrating clatter of the dark entities was now coming from that beat up structure positioned on the side of the stairway. I got on my hands and knees, crawled over to the other side of the steps, keeping my position as I peeked behind a set of honeysuckle bushes at the side of the house. I was terrified, but uncontrollably curious. I waited for something else to happen. I waited for more voices, but the entities seemed to be gone. I waited several minutes before I stood up. Still trembling and horrified, I walked backwards up the stairs still facing the old house, still much afraid of what still might be there. Only when I reached the top of the steps, I turned around then darted like a bludgeon animal, and got out of there!

I ran each step with a lesser degree of fright and began to realize that I was still surrounded by unexplainable presences and probably always would.

I kept that, along with numerous experiences from my mother, I thought she would overreact or not react at all. My paranormal experiences were becoming *very* common as the months passed.

As mentioned before, Bisbee was made from acts of glory and disgrace. The stories told by history books and community family members have many discrepancies about the legacy of the mining camp. But, nevertheless, they are very interesting and may explain why so many men, women, and children departed from this world in dismay, and still reside there, in some form or another.

Now, don't get me wrong. Bisbee has not only built itself on scenes of trauma, but the family tree of old town also prides itself on moral values. Life in early Bisbee had young, joyous pioneers that came from all over the world, to build successful lives in the booming mine camp. They came here with the same virtuous ideals that built this part of the southwest that so many can be proud of. But the side of the copper mining community that showed disappointing actions will be covered due to the stronger connection associated with supernatural sightings.

My coverage of Bisbee's history not only includes the young and old prostitutes but also includes lively characters and corrupted miners who have left clear psychic flashes in several sites. Incredible stories told by my mother, grandmother, and various aunts and uncles gave me insight of early Bisbee and all of its health problems.

They said tribulations such as disgusting green slime water flowing down the gulch, caused from the rows and rows of houses put on wooden stilts and built on the man- made terraces on Chihuahua Hill, directly above Brewery Gulch was one of the worst. The sewage or lack of, was the demon and cause of horrible living conditions, and the slime.

So many men and woman became ill due to the health situation, ranging from the elderly to infants. During the Gulch's hey-days, my mother said that the Gulch was tagged as a horrible place of disease and at the time, shouldn't be visited.

Monsoon rains brought extreme devastation to the entire community of Bisbee many times over. Raging waters have flowed down the Canyon and through Brewery Gulch, leaving broken and shattered miner's cabins, and wooden homes to newly homeless citizens.

I have personally seen the deep ditches of the Canyon over flow, and modern-day cars float on their roofs, down the middle of the Gulch. I have witnessed two local horses get stuck in one of the higher ravines of Tombstone Canyon, lose their footing, and actually get caught in the flow of the running rain water!

The community of Bisbee is deeply nestled in the Arizona mountains of the southwest. A place that is arid and dry for most of the year, and when the rains finally come, depending on the lack of moisture, can be a perfect setup for severe flooding.

On many occasions, this type of rain has taken the lives of several people. Drowning in the ditches of Bisbee used to be more common than it is today. Education of safety and common sense has justified the significant decrease of lives caused by flooding waters.

Because of the tight fit of residential and business spaces, just like in the present day, Bisbee was constantly facing the threat of fire. During the first decade of Bisbee's existence, a horrible fire erupted and demolished the entire business district. Years later, my grandmother said Chihuahua Hill was completely lost to an out of control inferno, leaving residents with out homes, again.

These surprising scenes of terror and overwhelming sadness brought a cloud of depression among its citizens. These forces of strange twists of destiny drew a power from all who were touched by the experiences. The influence of depression gained its momentum as each incident of tragedy played out.

This strange fog has formed itself into an entrance from the past into the present seeming to leave supernatural impressions of destruction felt by several of current day residents.

Despite early complications, individuals still flocked here. Bisbee's Copper Mine had produced more than eight billion pounds of copper which, in my opinion is a fabulous achievement made by every single generation of miners who excavated the minerals from the depths of the earth. This tremendous amount of success gives a demonstration of the sincerity felt by the townspeople for the American dream.

The life of a young psychogenic, with extrasensory perception whose mind was filled with various degrees of fear and anxiety, was at times very difficult to deal with. The others, who are beginning to feel the forces of psychic forces, will all react in various degrees of expectations. It depends on the strength of the child's awareness of the different messages sent from the 'other side': The urge to answer and the ability to resist the calls of the dead; if the entity comes in a dark form of energy or with scores of questions barking from its purple-colored lips, the raw electricity can drive a young child completely mad.

A parent, guardian, or mentor, must take to heart when a babe tells them of strange experiences that are unexplainable. A young soul can become confused to the reality of this world and *there's*, forcing a tear in the membrane of eternity and living beings.

There was and still is a park filled with cement and surrounded by a black iron fence below my house in the Gulch. The 'City Park' was actually Bisbee's first cemetery before becoming a recreation spot. At the street free side of the park is another set of concrete stairs, numbering around 75. Here, a small child often visited me from the next world.

I often entered the park through entrance of the steps, where we would often bump heads. He wasn't a mischievous creature, but instead very bossy.

I was never fearful of the odd playmate, but felt he was protecting hollow ground. Historians write the tactful move of the graves to the new cemetery (Evergreen Cemetery) before the new landscape of the park began. So we know that there are no body-filled-coffins under the concrete floor of City Park. Even so, I was flashed pictures of a young male, in blue jacket and short pants showing me his mother's grave.

"Here, she lies...asleep, girl. This is blessed soil; a place not for ragged children to run and to skip over, " conveyed the young entity.

I instead chose not to cross the *gravesite* again. To this day, I enter the park through the other two entrances.

Murderous acts of violence depict the past of Bisbee; during the time I speak is one of tremendous horror. The most dramatic of stories, told with truthful detail by uncles and generations of community families, tell about the five men who decided to rob the place where the payroll of the Copper Queen mine was delivered and kept. This unraveled, just years after the town's discovery and development.

The clatter of firing handguns began approximately at sunset, a small group of men rode up the Gulch on horseback and dismounted before arriving on Main Street, were holy hell erupted. As two masked men stood guard outside the establishment of the Goldwater and Castaneda store, three others entered shooting.

At the height of the gunfight, an individual came upon the battle and began to shoot at the robbers, right in the middle of Main Street.

My uncle said that a pregnant woman, a woman who owned stores in Bisbee, and three other men were killed, from the flying lead jetting through the narrow street.

Rumor had it that the group of gunslingers made refuge in the Chiricahua Mountains, where soon after, were caught and put in the Cochise County jail, located at the time in Tombstone. The criminal group of men was sentenced to killed by hanging, but there was a twist to the story. A sixth man was involved. He was the brain of the thieving plan, but not an actual corporeality of the robbery and killings.

My relative said that the townspeople of Bisbee were not happy with the decision of the jury in Tombstone. They apparently decided to sentence him to life-imprisonment, and not death. Bisbee was, and in small ways, still is a tight-knit community, and with this spirit of the newly developed town, chose to meet together in Tombstone. They walked in a mob, to the brainchild of the murdering gang's cell.

Here, Bisbee townspeople and miners forced their way into the criminal's cell and forced jails' men to hand him over to their enraged hands. The terrified man was tied and led from his cell down Toughnut Street just above First Street, in Tombstone, becoming a victim of public lynching, avoiding a lifetime in prison. The other men were hanged as planned.

"That crazy guy was buried in 'Boothill.' Serves him right," said my uncle.

The way the gang and who was involved was killed is a sad, sad, demonstration of the times, and a dreadful time of memory for the community of Bisbee.

These exact scenes of terrifying deaths are examples of souls being plummeted into another spectrum, causing a calamity of direction by spirit and free will.

These types of murders, including the hangings, are vile and foul. They pronounce the victim into complete blackness, making the path to the light hard to take sight of.

Many Bisbee natives of numerous generations have said, "During the wee-hours of the night, on Main Street, you can hear the many voices of those who were lost in the most terrible ways."

The weeping cries of depressed, lost souls, sweeps the historic neighborhoods of Bisbee in the darkest of night, calling to those, who will hear and to those strong enough to believe in their existence. An existence left in a small corner of the world, earthbound for indefinite time.

Chapter VI

The visions, sounds, and mental flashes from another realm, seemed to increase as my young life ran its course of sad and disturbing experiences. The realization of being a medium began to set in, so did the connection between trauma and free energy. It seemed the more stressed I felt, the more I experienced. As my own uneasiness engulfed my living soul, the flow of supernatural electricity increased as well.

The period of minor depression and hark knocks experienced through the teenage years, paints a time of elaborate incidents and haunting memories.

Over the course of my adolescence, my parents separated and reunited several times. They were very stubborn and dramatic in their appeals. My parents were very much in-love, but such as several other couples, got tired of one another's habits. So, every so often, my mother kicked my father out of the house and pounded the pavement for a minimum-wage job.

At one time, my mother went to an extreme degree and moved my family into a rundown apartment in the Warren District of Bisbee (with the exception of my three sisters who chose to room together in a nearby apartment). My mother was holding a full-time cook position at the 'Miners Diner,' a popular restaurant in Old Bisbee. She managed to work out a child support system with my father, whom I only saw once during the five-month separation period.

We had what we needed, food, an occasional trip to the clothes stores, and a roof over our heads. My older brother, Alfred, was busy planning his high school graduation while juggling a work schedule at the local ice cream shop. While Mother and he worked, I was left in charge of my younger brother Albert. Despite the constant presence of my kid brother, I spent much time alone in my own room.

My mother and Albert shared a room, while Alfred had his and I had my own individual space. Alfred's was located in the front of the apartment, near the living room. His room was completely wood paneled with a dark and thickly varnished material. The tiny, one windowed room had a small closet, which later proved to possess more than clothes.

Upon an early Saturday morning, my mother ventured out with Albert in tow, for a morning of grocery shopping while Alfred was at work. I insisted on staying home to watch the appearance of one of my favorite bands on the morning teen/dance television show.

I enjoyed the quietness of an empty home and sat at the end of the living room couch closest to Alfred's room, waiting patiently for the much anticipated television guest, I sipped on a cold glass of orange juice and judged the dancers on the show with a critical eye.

I was interrupted by a loud scream coming from just outside the apartment building. I immediately shot up from my seat and ran to the front window to see what was causing the uproar.

I slowly pulled the sheared curtains apart to clear my view and couldn't see anything suspicious. I turned around to turn down the volume of the television, which was just in my reach. I returned my concentration back to the window and scanned the outside.

Since my apartment was on the second floor, I had the view of the entire corner of the neighborhood and didn't see anyone on the street.

"Strange," I said out loud.

I turned up the volume of the television and peculiarly enough on the way to the couch I heard another strange reverberation. This time the source of another strange noise was coming from Alfred's room. It was the faint sound of a person breathing. I froze in my tracks and turned my head in the direction of the eerie noise.

"Who's there?" I pleaded.

No reply.

I listened with strained ears as the sound continued with louder tones. I decided to tiptoe slowly and as quietly as I could to the room's entrance. As the strange sounds rolled on, my heart began to increase its speed of blood delivery. My skin crawled as the hair stood on end.

Frightened but curious, I moved closer into the doorway of Alfred's unoccupied room listening for the direction in which the rhythms of breathing were coming. As the inhalations became louder, it was clear the eeriness was coming from the bedroom closet.

Suddenly the focus of energy attracted me directly toward the closed door of the clothes cabinet. I found myself lured to the middle of the room starring at the door. The breathing intensified and my terror increased to a point of being out-of-control. I soon felt the tears roll down my face as I tried to keep some kind of composure.

Without warning, mental flashes of a horrific scene were shown to me by an unknown force. A small man was crouching closely to the floor, tightly holding his head with both hands, crying in deep sobs. His chest and back were shaking as he obviously struggled to suck in the air into his lungs.

His nose dripped with runny mucus. He looked up at me, but said nothing. He then quickly fell to his knees and began to grab and pull at his shirt collar, as if he were choking. His face was rapidly turning a deep shade of red, then purple. I could see the veins bulging from his forehead as a puss looking substance began to spurt from the sides of his mouth.

I tried to shake my own head in some kind of desperation to stop the disgusting scene. It didn't work. I was forced to watch the petite man continue with his physical pain.

All of sudden, I could see what was causing his choking. A dark, thick smoke was incredibly apparent due to a horrendous fire that was creeping around the doorway of the closet!

"Stop! Stop it now!" I screamed. "Please, please…I don't want to see any more!"

The fire was now burning the clothes above the man.

"I can't help you! I can't!" I screamed out loud.

I was now on the floor with knees and my head flat to the ground in complete hysteria. Feeling exhausted and completely drained, I finally stopped crying and realized the mental pictures had stopped.

I sat up and became aware of the complete quietness of the room.

I slowly pushed my body to a standing position as I kept my eyes on the closet door. I didn't hear the breathing anymore. I wiped my tears and dare not look away, fearful of the man behind the door.

I shook my head again, from side to side, trying to shake off the revolting pictures that were just flashed to me. I closed my eyes and rubbed off any droplets of tears left on my cheeks, and took in a deep, slow breath, holding it for a few seconds before letting it out. I regained my composure and opened my eyes, then took a careful step forward.

Only after taking another long and penetrating breath, I proceeded with another step closer to the door. When I reached for the doorknob, I smelt a faint, vapor of smoke. I looked down toward my feet and witnessed a black cloud of smoke abruptly climbing toward my face.

"Oh my God! Are you still in there?" I instinctively wrapped my hand around the doorknob and tried to open the door.—"Ouch!" The metal was hot! I continued to try to open it despite the heat, but it wouldn't budge!

I pulled and jiggled the door with all my might. The smell of burning flesh was now coming from under and around the sides of the door! I stepped back and covered by mouth and nose, gagging and coughing. In between my involuntary reactions, I screamed for someone to help me.

Unexpectedly, The closet door whipped open and pushed me back onto the floor. As I fell, I crashed into the corner of bed and hit my head on the metal part of the frame. I reached for my injury and looked up toward the closet. Surprisingly, the closet was empty, with the exception of unscathed clothes and shoes. The smoke and choking man had disappeared.

That grossly intense experience was the first of a string of supernatural occurrences I suffered, during a high anxiety period of my young life. The link between a magnitude of tension and a broader openness to the spiritual realm is a self-inspired theory of intensified paranormal sensitivity.

When a person, young or old experiences some type of personal strain, they may unknowingly be opening themselves up to a disheartened spirit, widening the access to the paranormal world, and also strengthen the transmitting single to this world.

I believe the energy usually connected with the living source of a person's emotional state can spark a dawning interest, especially if sadden, to an earthbound spirit. The spirits can feed off our own living energy, especially when it is heavy with depression or anger.

The entity that clings to an area that was their place of traumatic death or maybe a cherished place of peaceful meditation will also adhere to a weakened moral fiber. The paranormal will pick-up on the living souls difficulty, choosing to generate from the sad energy, sometimes causing an uncoordinated collection of raw energy. A solemn, gentle banshee may become a poltergeist due to the prolonged gloom of the person they are clinging too.

Poltergeist activity: Doors unexpectedly slamming shut; objects mysteriously falling from shelves and tables; electrical appliances being turned on and off, when no one is near them; all just examples of an empowered entity.

Yes, these may happen when a household is joyous, but it will increase when deep sorrow clouds the space of the being. One mustn't be nonsensical about the stir-up of mischievous spirits in a grief-struck home. The depressed individual may be pulled into a deeper and more painful state, by the haunting entity. The more stress, anger, and sadness demonstrated by a person, the more intense the paranormal activity may become.

The self-inspired theory of involuntary mediation, with unrest spirits, comes straight from my real-life experiences. As a young, often overly stressed teenaged-girl, who was trying to deal with adolescence and a very dysfunctional family life, I often put myself into an 'open state' of the psyche. A perfect set up for an unsolicited invitation from the paranormal.

Before I drifted off to sleep, in the same apartment of the burning closet, I was often afraid with a profound and stabbing fear, painfully staying inside me. The physical pain tied to intense stress and worry often woke me during the darkest point of night. An abnormal perspiration would force my eyes open to the complete stillness of hours of darkness.

Many times I remember waking to gray shadows surrounding my twin-sized bed. I was always in the fetal position, lying on my left side, clutching my gold crucifix, and freezing my position for hours. Even during sleep, I was calling the Angels of God to help me fight whatever was surrounding my bed and disturbing my young life.

They seemed to show up in two's and three's when I was at lowest. When my life was running smoother and more carefree, visitors from the supernatural world would be less frequent.

After some time of living in that second level apartment, my parents reunited. We moved into a house up the same street. Unfortunately, the abundance of paranormal visitors did not stop, despite the fact of my parents living back together.

I was now in the middle of my 8th grade year and still dealing with constant eruptions of warring parents. The string of haunting visitors continued and more mental flashes were revealed to me.

This one particular time a female entity contacted me with a sad, heartrending story. Ironically, another narrative including an inferno and lonely death was exemplified.

In the small, two-bedroom, one level house, occupied by my parents, Albert and myself, I oddly smelt and on occasion, saw the fog of a strange smoke drifting from above the kitchen. My dog Pepper, at the time (I have had several dogs over the years) would constantly howl and screech during the same time as my strange encounters. These engagements with the unknown seemed somehow different and succeeded to pull me into another level of the psyche.

It was during a quiet, late afternoon, on a cool, autumn day, I lye on my bed studying for a social study test scheduled for the next day, when I experienced a strange panorama.

I was heavily involved in my books and listening to my favorite music, barely aware of my surroundings, when I was feverishly interrupted. The sounds of a faint sobbing came from the kitchen, on the other side of my doorway. I thought it was my younger brother at first, but then I remembered he was at a friend's house.

I returned to my homework, but the room continued to slowly fill with an eerie mood. Suddenly, my nervousness was turned to terror. My hands were clammy and my pulse ran fast. I took a deep breath, but began to curiously cough as my eyes began to suspiciously burn as well.

I threw my pencil down and pushed my books off the bed as I quickly stood up. I headed toward the two, large closed windows on the other side of the room. I clumsily tried to push open the painted shut panes, as I continued my strange coughing.

Still struggling with the windows, I heard the voice of a strange woman. Her medium toned voiced, faintly called out to me.

"There is no way out..."

I snapped my neck around toward the voice, but seeing no one. I quickly produced tears and began to scream for help as the mysterious voice continued its strange anthem.

"You can't get out. I told you...there is no way out."

The voice, the smoke, and my out-of-control behavior were suddenly struck down in an instant as my mother walked into the room.

"What is going on in here?" she hollered.

"I don't know. Can you smell the smoke?" I said in-between breaths.

"Smoke? What? No."

"That's why I was trying to do open the windows and why I was…coughing."

At that point, I realized the room was clear of any presence of smoke and my throat felt fine. I walked back to my books and pencil spread on the floor and without looking at my mother, I said, "I'm sorry. I guess I just got hot."

My mother simply turned around and walked out of the room. I stood in complete stillness and blurted out a somber cry. The encounter left me with an impression of pure dread. I didn't even attempt to tell my mother, since the days of the Tombstone Canyon house, she didn't dare mess with that sort of thing anymore. It was if she closed her paranormal abilities off, once and for all.

As the following weeks passed, I couldn't shake my own personal despair, and felt the desperation of the strange female voice. When it was time to sleep, I was often awoken by a soft and easy weight on the end of my bed. At first I would instinctively pop open by eyes and left my head to see whom in the world would be on my bed in the middle of the night. When I affixed my eyes in the dim light, I saw no one. After a few times of this happening, I decided to just let it be and try not to catch a glimpse.

As the days and nights drifted by, and the visitations at the end of my bed increased, so did my grief. The more nights of haunting interruptions that passed, the more sadden I became. It was if the night visitor was trying to fill my young soul with her own ill-willed feelings.

During a heightened time of my despair, the picture of the sad spirit's death was shown to me. During one of the entity's nighttime visits, I saw her life flash, picture by picture, from the time of young women hood to her time of death.

I was forwarded to the house I was presently living in. The structure was not the same. It was a two-story home and the area above the kitchen was a bedroom decorated with various movie stars from the thirties and forties. (Even though I was merely thirteen, I was still able to recognize Cary Grant and Humphrey Bogart.)

The room was decorated plainly, but still seemed homey. As I was being lead by an invisible guide, I was suddenly shoved in front of a frail bodied woman. She looked at me straight in the eyes. Her face drawn and her dark circles around her eyes were definite. The sickly looking woman's hair was tangled and greasy. She wore a long, and yellow flowered-print nightgown and stood before me in her bare feet.

She turned away from me to face the bed positioned behind her. Now incapacitated by my presence, she walked toward a chair that matched her vanity, directly under a ceiling wood beam.

As she put her naked foot on the chair, I looked up toward the beam again and saw a noose hanging from it. The woman seemed melancholy as she stood there on the chair, looking straight ahead. Then she hung her head down as she positioned her hands in prayer. I heard her mumbling as she brought her hands to the rope hanging down inches in front of her face.

I wanted to stop her, but I couldn't speak nor move.

I noticed a small candle burning on the makeup desk; its flame flickered back and forth as the woman continued her deadly venture. With a noose tightly in place, the nameless person snapped her head toward my direction. Her stringy hair jolted and covered her left eye as she gazed at me with piercing, cold eyes. The corners of her mouth slowly pulled to a sarcastic grin as she quickly kicked the back of the chair she was standing on.

The swing, of her now lifeless body, was hard enough to push over the lit candle on the vanity. A transparent, peach colored, scarf hanging on the corner of the makeup desk's mirror began to savagely burn as the dead body continued to swing. I watched the woman in the light of the fire and was shaken from that moment in time and pushed back into the present.

After that intuitive experience, I realized I was falling into a strange state of depression. It was if the sad woman was somehow trying to pull me down to her level of self-pity.

I was not going to end up like that crazed person. I stopped feeling sorry for myself, gathered prayer pamphlets from my local church, which I obsessively read over and over. I memorized each prayer printed in between its covers with incredible interest, searching for an answer, and a glimmer of light.

I prayed every night as a way to fall asleep, and soon, the visits from the spirit-woman stopped. I realized many things after that frightful experience. The troubled relationship between my parents did not involve me, and any troubles I had at school were not as devastating as I had imagined.

Through my prayers, a new positive outlook to the world was given, and the female phantom was pushed away from my brightly, lit, soul. I had closed her entrance into my rejuvenated spirit and became a happy and peaceful individual.

Once and awhile I still felt her presence, but not like before. My emotional weakness let the entity disturb me in an unhealthy way. I promised myself I would never let that happen again. Never let those from beyond, pull me into their mystical state and endanger my mental and spiritual peace. A skill I was learning as I accepted the life as a clairvoyant and as a person different from many.

Let the emotional energies of disturbed entities slip from your grips, as you heal your own heart and strengthen your mind. Whatever may be disturbing your peace of mind, understand it will pass. Learn how to take life's improprieties with a grain of salt. Take the knowledge of each depressing moment in your life as a hard earned lesson, ready to use those times as a defense for the next complicated situation in your existence.

When you use this basic strategy, you will learn how to block out the negative energies of an entity inhabiting your current place of rest. When the lost soul feels your own spirit growing strong after an emotional fall, it will either feel the positive direction of your life or feed off of that good energy; or it will simply turn away from you.

This is a constructive approach to life in general, but most beneficial if you feel the presence of an arrogant poltergeist. To become a reinforced spirit of positive attitude in time of crisis will bring anyone out of any degree of depression, and placing the spirit and mind in a righteousness position.

The strength in affirmative reflection is beyond the potency of a sad, lonely entity, trying to prey on a weak and tired living soul. More vigor comes from the constructive and determined, spreading positive energy from within, and around his/her environment.

If we can remind ourselves, as often as we can, that we all have a short time on this earth and must live each and every moment with positive contemplation, we would be much better off.

Chapter VII

Days would pass into months, and then into years without a minute filled with unproductive, depressing, emotional stress. The breathing of the variety of hallow souls tapping my shoulder was bringing my young mind to near madness. *They* never left me to rest. The sarcasms of the lost spirits were now realizing my 'beam of light' was becoming strong and more energizing.

The various visitations I experienced continued into my young adulthood. It seemed in every house, apartment, or place of business a lingering aroma of death was inhaled by my living spirit. I began to learn to suck in the faint impressions of a past existence, a body that had ceased to function on this planet, leaving the stink of a stubborn spirit, unwilling to penetrate the membrane of eternal life.

I was passed the realization of my psychic ability, but now coming to grips with the power of my gift. The frequencies of the lost souls were beginning to come in clearly than before.

At times the waves of past lives were coming at an out-of-control speed. I couldn't control the raw energies of the countless lost spirits entering my personal place of serene consciousness, impossible at this stage of life.

The scenes of past lives replaying themselves are eerie reminders of every single person on this planet and their destiny. Including how they will be born into this world, with high or low class, and how they will die, peacefully or tragically.

After each encounter with the supernatural, I learned momentous lessons. Each banshee who came into contact with my own young, lively spirit left me with impressions of various types of knowledge concerning my purpose in life, and what I should do with it.

Now, in my early-twenties, I began to know who I was, better and better each passing day. Life in general is ironically filled with long points of meaning and hard to interpret. The center of individual preference to choose the way of living out experiences while on this earth is 'free will'. If one lets decisive moments creep past, the heart and mind will harden with unsatisfactory results of denied happiness. Causing a 'domino effect' of let down's and revenge filled thoughts blurring the path to inner peace.

The scenes of individual lives were etched by the intellectualist Himself, way before the person's birth, which are writings of the Lord, stories of scenes that with or without your consent will be played out.

The flashes of scenes herald to me are geared emotions of loneliness and regret, keeping the lost souls tied with the same tormenting emotional roller coaster, torturing them by not crossing completely over. Examples of stubbornness and ignorance can be evaded before a living spirit ceases by making a plain decision throughout life, to live as a complete instrument of God.

To succeed in His set forth destiny and to follow your true heart and gut feelings as you walk through the gardens of life, whether the gardens are filled with beautiful flowers and fruits, thriving under the sweet sunshine; or covered with weeds and dry, thorny vines under thick clouds; proceed with blind faith toward a successful harvest of life.

At the end of the life, do no fight death as you begin to see the gates of heaven. Do not turn your eyes back toward earth, in an attempt to retract your mistakes or guilt. Avoid the drama of rejecting your own foreordained death, or you too will become a roaming entity.

Follow the beam of God's grace as you encounter the time of death. All will be fine, only when you choose to leave this earth under the direction of God, and not turning an idiotic turn toward your own selfish reasoning in trying to stay…here.

You must take the chance to leave this planet with the faith of our 'Higher Power' then and only then, will the living spirit rest and find peace.

Legends of various cultures telling stories of haunting encounters with unearthly beings are passed from generation to generation, keeping the geste align in memory. One as such, is about a woman of the Mexican culture, called 'El Llorona' (the weeping one). There are quite a few variations of this Mexican record of a tormented soul, but this is the version I have been told by my Mexican/American relatives:

She was the mother of five small children and wife of a well-known, unfaithful man, whom, during one rain-filled night, was found in the arms of another.

At the very moment of seeing her husband wrapped in the lust of a stranger, she went completely insane.

Her actions were astounding. Instead of attacking the adulterers, she chose to turn from the sight and run directly home.

As the broken woman entered her tiny shack, she began to wail uncontrollably, turning every piece of furniture upside down. She screamed profanities as she tore the sleeves of her worn blouse, and then threw her thin wedding band into the fireplace as she kicked over the hurricane lamp on the dining table, causing a burst of flames to erupt in the middle of the room.

Then...she suddenly stopped and stood perfectly still. Taking in long penetrating breaths, while she held tight fists at each side of her hips.

El Llorona then fell to the ground and began to hit the wooden floor with her balled up hands, shaking her long, coarse, gray hair into a whirlwind of rage. Then slowly she stopped her tantrum and stood up, turning her red face and glossed-over eyes toward her trembling children standing in the corner of the room.

The psychotic woman let out a long and demonic scream then started to grab and holler at them, as she slapped and pulled at their arms and hair.

Falling to the ground with exhaustion, she began to mumble strange words in a whispering tone. Then the mad woman ordered her children to follow her outside. Once the smallest child was out, she jerked him by his left arm and threatened to break his neck if the rest didn't follow.

She dragged them all to the raging river near her house. As the storm terrorized the dark night with heavy rain and blinding lightening strikes, the enraged woman then threw each babe into the furious water, screaming and crying as they hit the white liquid!

After the horrific deed was done she quickly realized what she had done. She watched helplessly on the bank from above as her children began to drown. They called to her for rescue until finally, the mother watched her children's limp bodies float down the rapid river, dead.

Now, with nothing to live for, she too, threw herself into the same fatal water, thus ending the night terror at last.

Now, the spirit of El Llorona travels the desert in search of her murdered children, crying, sobbing, and screaming as the night wind carries her mournful wails across the golden landscapes. The sad entity glides low and close to the ground searching for the souls of her murdered children. Trying to catch a glimpse of a child, and at times mistakes living children as her own.

The most daggering recollection of El Llorona is the time I spent a night, along with my two small daughters (at the time) and sister Sally, at my dad's house in Douglas. My father had gone to bed early that autumn evening, falling asleep about the same time as my girls did. Dad was snoring lowly and alone in his bedroom, while Brittany and Chelsie were lying peacefully asleep on separate couches. A quiescent scene.

The night was unusually dark and dreadfully quiet and still. After watching a movie on TV, I took my place on the living room floor and wrapped myself in a sleeping bag. Just as I was on the verge of fading into the first stages of sleep I heard a cry in the distance. At first I thought it was a howling dog but then the sound came closer and louder. I heard Sally from a back bedroom say, "Fran, do you hear that?"

The wailing was quickly upon the house and before I could utter a word, Sally was already entering the living room.

The horrible and eerie cry of the demonic banshee was awesome! She seemed to scream into the front open living room window, positioned directly in front of me!

I could feel her demented energy pushing at the glass, as she tried to enter the house!

"Oh, my, God! Fran, go to Brittany! I'll go to Chelsie! Mom used to say if El Llorona is near small kids, she will try to take them!" Sally said with trembling voice. "But, she can't break the bond of a mother and her child," she added.

I did as she said, as she scurried over to Chelsie, her Godchild. We sat as close to the children as we possibly could without waking them up, listening to the bloodcurdling screams of the haunting mistress outside.

The sound of the being, traveled from window to window, screaming and wailing louder with each passing second. The girls surprisingly did not wake up despite the entity's ear cracking screams.

El Llorona moved to the back of the house and continued her cries at the rear door. Sally and I prayed *The Lord's Prayer* out loud. The sinister wraith returned to the front porch and went to the first window where she first started her deafening moans. We in turn, prayed even louder and harder, drowning out her loud cries.

Finally, after a good five minutes, her weeping tones traveled around to the other side of the house and faded down the alley, toward the backyard. Eventually, her voice was gone, along with her hellish energies.

That really was one the most memorable encounters spued from the supernatural world I have ever experienced! The depressed spirit of El Llorona is and will most likely roam this earth long after my great, great-grand children will walk this earth. The guilty condition of El Llorona thrashes and darkens as each exhibition of finding her children ends in vain. How horrible to be trapped in such a deplorable state of consciousness and deep suffrage, seemingly forever.

Is the story of this crazed woman an example of an unjust faith in God a lesson for all to see? Will this demonic soul scare an unsuspected mortal into the reality of the supernatural?

I believe God allows certain appeals of unanswered requests for the benefit of others. If just one person can hear the horrible desperation of the spirit I am referring too, then maybe that experience will save his or her own soul from such a scenario. Take this chastisement as a warning from God as a chance to repent from the evils of self-sin and immoral judgment.

The town of Douglas was another site for my supernatural experiences, highlighted at the historical 'Gadsden Hotel' located on G Avenue. This high-rise hotel holds the rights to the infamous story of 'Pancho Villa' turn-of-the-century rebel, who is said to have: "...rode his breathtaking steed into the lobby with both six-shooters firing as he raced up and down the marbled staircase, enumerating words of war and freedom..." The incredible visual of a vigilante is the sign of its time.

This site is also a magnet to many, many claimed psychics, answering to vibes of several entities inhabiting the hotel. The owners have been quoted to saying that most 'incidents' happen during the Christmas season.

Several and various occurrences tied to unexplainable events have played out in the ancient building. Hotel maids over the years have individually alleged to have been slapped in the face by an invisible attacker; doors opened and slammed by themselves; muffled cries and shrieks came from empty rooms; all documented incidents from many visitors over decades of public usage.

During the year of 1987, while working as a Hostess for the hotel's restaurant, I was asked to help out one of the busboys. He was assigned 'room service' duty and was rushed with regular customers. The head waitress asked if I would deliver a lunch tray, as the young boy tried to keep up with the afternoon crowd.

I gladly accepted the assignment and took the tray of one cheeseburger, fries, a bowl of vanilla ice cream, and a large coke to the third floor.

As I waited for the hotel guest to answer my knock at the door, I naturally looked out the window at the end of the hall. I noticed the see-through curtains were a bit dusty and the window slightly cracked in the lower right corner. The patriot was taking his or her time, making me realize the weight of the heavy plate and glass.

"*Hey...hey...*" whispered a stranger.

I turned my head toward the voice, without moving my body from its position. All I saw was the empty hallway, and knocked on the door again.

"*Hey...hey...*" repeated the voice.

This time I turned completely around and said, "Excuse me. Who's there? Can I help you?"

I heard footsteps coming toward me, but not a person in sight.

"Hello? Who's there?" I repeated nervously.

My arms and legs began to tremble. I turned around and began to knock at the door and hollered, "Lunch is here. Open up, please!"

I didn't want to turn around again, paranoid to see what was coming my way. The hall became incredibly cold. The shiny floor seemed to vibrate as the voice of the invisible stranger continued, "*Hey...Hey...*" "—I am so sorry Miss. I was in the shower. I didn't hear your knocking. I am starving!" said the middle-aged woman as she swung open the hotel door.

I let a big sigh of relief, as I said, "No problem, ma'am, it was a pleasure."

"Thank God for room-service. How much will it be?" asked the hotel guest.

"Oh, let me check the ticket. With dessert, it comes to $4.50."

"Ok, sweetie. Here is a five. Keep the change!"

I thanked the woman and turned toward the stairway. I didn't want to wait for the elevator. I hurriedly made it down the steps, feeling as if I were being followed. The minute I landed on the last step, I felt at ease. Whatever was following me couldn't overshoot the stairway.

What fires-up the memory of a lost soul and what was it about me knocking at the door with a full servicing tray that caused the entity in the hotel to talk to me? What in general sparks the thoughts of a recurring memory to play its self over and over?

To understand the world of a lost soul includes questions gearing toward their own reasoning of making themselves earthbound, and why they choose to haunt their last place of physical presence. Are they just confused or do they know exactly what they are doing?

Who asks the same questions as myself? Believers and nonbelievers? The religious and irreligious?

Present times have come back to spirituality and opened hearts and minds to infinite possibilities of what might be. Citizens of today's society are uncanny to past legends by dissecting those stories with technical and modern electronics, measuring such things as 'cold spots' and magnetic areas of the earth, probable causes of paranormal activities.

These in my view are a good and a progressive step in the right direction. It is good to ask questions of the spiritual sense. It brings you closer to God. As in all generations and through pages of time, questions of life and what happens after death is a continued event. Do heaven and hell really exist? Is there a place in-between? The actual transition from the earthly world to the afterlife has sparked the interest of many and with it has intensified more questions regarding the subject than ever before.

If you take a positive approach to the ancient questions of life after death you will be intrigued by the journey and be taken to places that you have never probably explored before. This concept will motivate you into finding ways of opening up to an exciting and interesting place of the psychic world, and maybe along the way, release some of the fear associated with the supernatural.

The cynical and unbelievers are just as lost as those spirits floating in and out of consciousness in structures and streets of Old Bisbee and other sites surrounding our planet. What will bring these lost souls to the reality? What will satisfy them into the truth? What will make those who are still in the living world believe and realize they have the ability to send lost souls in the right direction toward eternal peace?

Will *they* ever wake up?

Chapter VIII

Now a mother of two daughters, has my sensitivity to the paranormal increased? I feel as I've aged through life, my openness to the super naturalistic aspect of the universe has broadened. I have fully accepted my gift as a receiver from souls who have been earthbound, taking in the energies with a more positive attitude.

My life as a pronounced medium is much more calm and not so terrifying as it was before. I understand my position in the psychic world much better then I did as a child, teen, or a young woman in her twenties. I have reached the mark of a late 'thirty something' woman, and ready at all times to go head to head with any paranormal commotion. I am a mother, and my children had over the course of their young lives demonstrated their own psychic abilities.

Since they could speak, they asked me very often, "Mom…you called me?" More often than not, I would look at them with raised eyebrows, and answer, "No, why?" Their usual reply, "Oh, I heard someone call me…"

These types of basic capabilities of the psychic nature were the beginnings of my own gift. My mother was a clairvoyant, as her mother. I truly believe it is a family blessing to have the ability to tune in on the electric waves of another realm.

To realize this as approbation from the grace of God may come very hard for some at first. All people do have the ability to open themselves to the spirit world, but just some of us are more attuned to do so. The possibility to be bequeathed the gift of psychic ability is very likely with one key thing to remember, one must accept a gift before enjoying it.

Rosters of paranormal encounters in different homes and towns in Arizona have fueled my supernatural talent. The state is the 'baby state' of the United States, but its history spans far more than the early days of the area becoming a Territory of the New Frontier.

As the east coast has New England, Boston, and Salem to prove notable events extending to days of the Mayflower, the west has the legends and stories of the desert to tell as well.

Over the red-rock canyons and Saguaro blanketed hillsides are the spirits of those who lived before the witches of Salem were burned at the stake. The dry, heated landscapes of the Arizona desert have scores of footprints belonging to generations of the Native American tribes, the Mexicans, and much later in time, the trail of the pioneers.

All of these together have woven a unique array of powerful energy traveling over the stillness of the desert. The stories of all who perished linger in the variety of outposts within the borders of its state lines, sharing chronicles of impeccable value ending in precarious circumstances.

In 1997, I, along with my young family was residing in Safford. A small community located in east-central Arizona. During that time we lived in a double-wide mobile home, about one mile from town and at the base of Mount Graham, home of the endangered species of the Red Squirrel, and an astrophysical site with the peak of approximately 10,720 feet.

According to local historians, Mt. Graham is located in the Pinaleño Mountains, taken from a Native American word meaning 'many deer.' The Apache people moved into the area of what is now Safford sometime in the 1600s. The reservation for the San Carlos Apache Tribe was formed in 1871, according to history literature.

Of course, some of the most revered Apache tribe members were Cochise and Geronimo, both from the Chiricahua Tribe and infamous in Arizona.

Mt. Graham has a lot of history with the Apache people…part of which I mentioned earlier; have inherited some of the bloodline from my paternal grandmother.

The landscape that surrounded the home we lived in at the time was quite beautiful. Cacti and desert wildlife were the view from all adjacent windows. At night, the cry of the coyotes acted like sweet songs of the west calling to his mate as the bright moon glowed over the somnolent backdrop.

During one of those desert evenings, Chelsie cried from her room, situated on the other side of the house. "Mommy! Mommy!"

At the same moment I had just climbed into bed and was pulling my comforter over my chest when I heard her sweet little voice.

"Mommmmy, come here!"

"What is it, Chelsie?" I yelled back.

I took in a deep breath and flung the bedspread off of me and sat up.

Suddenly a loud 'Kaboom' mad me whip my head toward the bedroom closet positioned on the right side of the room where the walk-in closet was located. I began to shake my husband, lying beside me and whispered, "Bill…did you hear that? Bill…"

Being a deep sleeper he didn't wake up and evidently didn't hear the crash on the other side of the closed storeroom either. As I focused my sight toward the noise, I was drawn through my mind's eye into the storage area. As I felt myself being pulled by a strange force, I began to see and hear the crickets of the night, as if I were now outside.

The smell of a burning fire was verified as I saw the blur of a large blaze in far distance, flaring higher and higher. The sounds of gentle drums were filling the night keeping a slow, rhythmic tempo.

The beats of the drums then suddenly changed too fast…then slow…mesmerizing me as they became louder and closer. My peripheral vision was blocked by strange darkness, keeping me focused on the flame. I could still hear the crackling of the fire, regardless of the loudness of the drums. The heat of the bonfire was not felt, but I could feel the presences of many strangers. The scenery seemed to turn in a slow circle around me. I could see the distorted images of several strangers facing toward me, as the colors of their clothes stretched into longer and longer blurs.

As I continued to spin, I realized the unfamiliar people began to move around with dance like motions, in tempo with the drums. Almost at the exact time of the strangers dance, a lone voice sang in a curious language, his voice sounding like a wailing long cry, high and drawn in beat with the drums. The singer was soon joined by two or three more voices, in the same pitch and dialect.

I stopped turning in circles and was pushed from behind to stand directly in front of two men whose eyes were as dark as the night. They stood motionless and as elegantly as two statues would, in front of a dome-shaped tent. One was dressed in a dark, long sleeved shirt and leather colored pants. He wore white beads, stringed over many times, all the way to the end of his shirt. Because of the brightness of the fire, I could see his dark brown skin and long hair, regardless of the obscurity of the night.

The other man was dressed completely in white. His jacket embroidered with colorful, shiny beads in the pattern of some type of flowering vine. His hair was dark and pulled back in the front. He had on a red sash, with fringed edges.

The men spoke no words. All I could hear now were the singers in the distance. The smell of the fire was penetrating my nostrils as I began to fill tightness in my chest. The drums were becoming more intense and grew astonishing loud. I instinctively grabbed at the area where it pained me and in my mediated state, fell to the ground, feeling the sharp rocks puncturing my knees. Then I looked up at a new group of men, except they were wearing some type of face covering, peering down at me…

"Mommy! I don't feel good," cried Chelsie.

I was stunned! I was quickly pushed back into the present and regained my composure and directed my attention back to Chelsie. I got right out of bed and jogged toward her room turning on her light to investigate the problem.

"You feel sick, honey?"

"My tummy hurts. I feel like puking."

"Do you want some water?" I asked.

She nodded no and said, "Sleep with me, Mommy. Please."

"Only until you feel better or fall to sleep, okay?"

She nodded and grabbed my hand directing me to her side.

Chelsie fell asleep before feeling better, leaving me to spend the night in her room. Surprisingly, I was tired enough to forget where I was in the house and when a strange clatter of activity awoke me, I was instantly terrified. Since Chelsie's room was positioned on the other side of the two-car garage, the sound of one of the garage doors going up, then down, was considerably loud!

When I first heard the chains pulling the heavy door, I thought I was dreaming. Then it continued, repeatedly. I instinctively thought it was Bill, believing it was morning and he was going to the convenient store for a pack of cigarettes. But then I realized it was actually still night and I was sleeping in my daughter's room. I didn't know what to do next. I made sure my toddler didn't wake up and sat halfway up in the bed, listening. Before I got up and checked, Bill was calling my name.

"Fran! What are you doing?"

"Nothing! I'm in bed with Chelsie," I replied.

I saw him walk past the room I was in and heard him open the back door leading directly into the garage. The mysterious force continued to open and close the metal door as Bill began to pound the red button that controlled the mechanics.

"What the hell is going on here?" asked Bill.

Then, *it* stopped. Completely.

"Fran, did you hear that?" Bill asked as he stood outside of the bedroom door, with a puzzled face.

"Yes...Do you think something is wrong with the wiring?"

"I don't know. Why are you with Chelsie? Is she sick?"

"She said her stomach hurt, so I'm going to stay with her."

"Well, I'm going back to bed. 'Night," he said as he let out a big yawn.

The next morning, I asked my husband over a cup of coffee if he was scared the night before. As he put his lips on the ceramic mug, he shook his head no and rolled his eyes.

"Right." I said with a sarcastic tone.

"That was strange. But what is even stranger is what happened when I went to our bedroom," Bill said. "When I entered the bedroom I thought you were standing behind me and before I could turn around, I was pushed onto the bed, hard! I got mad and told you to cut it out, but when I turned my body around toward the door, you weren't there."

"What?" I said in astonishment.

"Yeah. I got pushed onto the bed. When I realized it wasn't you, I just took the covers and put them over my head!" He said with a slight laugh in is voice.

I took a deep breath and said, "There is something definitely going on. Actually, there is something I haven't told you about the closet in our room."

"What do you mean?" asked Bill.

"Well, you know how we keep our ironing board in there?"

He nodded.

I continued, "After a couple of nights I could hear a light bumping noise on one of the walls. I ignored it for a while, but a couple of days ago I shut the door before going to bed. After a couple of minutes of lying in bed, it sounded like the board got thrown against the closed door!"

"You're kidding!"

"No. I didn't feel like checking it out. I just stayed in bed, but in the morning when I opened the door the ironing board fell right on my toes! It freaked me out, since I put the thing against the furthest wall from the door."

The garage door episode passed with no more mention from either of us, but I couldn't forget the strange vision I saw of what it looked like to me was some sort of Native American gathering, of immense significance.

I was around many Apache people who lived at the San Carlos Reservation, which is fairly near Safford. Running into men and women, who were members of the reservation at places such as the local grocery store and at local high school sport functions, never grasping the idea that their ancestors were still very much alive in the spiritual sense, with a strong presence in the mountains and surrounding areas of my home, at the base of Mt. Graham.

I know the Apache people believe in the supernatural and leave their great sense of pride and love in the acres and acres of desert and mountain they left behind when they were 'free people.' The calling from the 'other side' was an incredible look into the world gone past of the Native American history filled with passion for nature and the respect given to those who have left this earth but are still present in the spiritual sense.

The call of the Native American voice can be heard in the natural whizz of the breeze, as it flows through the shiny leaves of the Cottonwood, or when it accompanies the intelligent cry of the coyote in the dark of the night. The wisdom of the people, who were 'captured' in the desert, is now free in the world of the supernatural.

According to recorded history, the Mule Mountains of Bisbee have been explored by a variety of people across time, first the Apaches, then the genealogists. These particular mountains are filled with deep canyons and Juniper brush, and the monumental peaks have the power of reminiscences of diligent impressions of past lives, waiting to be discovered. The narrow path of its earliest years, were so rocky and treacherous that it took the strength of mules to traverse the trails, hence the name, 'Mule Mountains.'

My mother said during the late 1950s, that the mountain was blasted and a tunnel was engineered for car explorers, called Mule Tunnel Pass. Instead of driving over the lower area of the mountain, which joins highway 80 to the town of Bisbee (a very curvy and tight artery, historically known for several vehicular deaths), travelers could now drive safe and from almost definite harm.

Drivers may still take the scenic route of the old highway, nicknamed 'The Divide' (referring to the Continental Divide, a monument on the top of the roadway states the peak being part of it), but traveling at a much slower speed.

Above the old highway, a dirt road leading up to the area called 'Juniper Flats,' will take you to another adventure of mountainous scenery. The climb is extremely steep, with room only for one car width, seeming to reflect those of the years during the time of the free Apache.

Upon many hikes up the treacherous mountain road, one might be so privileged to hear the jingles of the metal of a warrior's horse, or the presence of a long passed spirit that still thrives in a supernatural sense. One might also be able to tune into the cosmic energy of the floating hawks that so passionately guide in poetic circles above the mountain, as they seemingly check the soul signature of those who are deeply engraved in the mysteries of the western world and bonded with Mother Earth.

Chapter IX

One of the first prayers my daughters, Chelsie and Brittany, learned in Catechism was one devoted to the guardian angels. Taken from the True Catholic Website: *"Angel of God, My Guardian Dear, to whom His love commits me here, ever this day be at my side, to light and guard, to rule and guide."*

This invocation has a gentle and childlike tone that seems to grow into a peaceful rhythm, intoning divine words for the celestial beings. The ancient unities we call angels, have existed since the beginning of time and will surpass its end, leaving behind many legends, as well as myths, both dramatic and sweet. A perfect example of celestial legend is recounted in the tale I once heard, of how humans received the indentation above the lip and below the nose:

As the tiny babe begins to drift into a deep slumber, a guardian angel sings a sweet lullaby, kisses his own index finger and places it on the baby, as if to shush the child of its visit. This causes a shape resembling a holy finger above our mouths, a touching and moving example of the eminence of God's angels.

As we ramble through life, dangers and unbelievable situations can exhaust our own spirit. We must have help to strive through such tribulations of earthly life. I believe God sends members of his heavenly army to protect, guide, and to give companionship to the humankind.

Over time, many have believed that a war is being continuously fought in between heaven and earth, a clash flanked by the warriors of God and the demons from hell.

A dear friend, for whom I will call Holly, told me about a childhood memory involving such a demonstration. Holly had a very happy childhood remembering mostly good images of her early life.

But, this one time, as she played in her bedroom alone with her stuff animals and baby dolls, she recalled one of definite opposition. In her own words:

"I was dressed in my mother's fur stole, gloves, and high heels, skipping around my play wood-dining table, singing a popular song from the era. As I began to pour my favorite doll a cup of tea, I noticed several shadows on the wall near to the table. Deciding to ignore the unusual figures, I turned my attention to my big white Teddy Bear, pretending to feed him a cookie; until the shadows again caught my attention by darting from corner to corner. Suddenly, I was shoved very hard onto one of the tiny chairs, feeling like I had been grabbed and pushed down.

The shadows then seemed to jump off the wall and quickly form into a tight circle around my pretend tea party. At that moment, a remarkable collection of individual jets of light entered the room from the left; surrounding the table in the same manner as the strange shadows.

The miniature lights were glowing gold and white, resembling fuzzy balls that hovered, growing brighter and brighter, as the seconds passed. As the tiny lights shined in a golden ring formation above my head, I remember suddenly falling asleep. (As an adult, I realized I wasn't sleeping, but rather in a state of deep meditation.) I was awakened from my meditative state by the screams of my mother.

I awoke to the violent shakes from my mother's hands and to the terror and the tears that flowed from her alarmed expression. I honestly don't remember what happened during my state of meditation, but my mother told me what she saw.

She said she was reading in her den when an unusual noise coming from my bedroom interrupted her. As she made her way to my room, the sounds increased in volume, causing her to run down the hall. As she neared the room, my mother heard my tiny voice change into a stronger and unfamiliar pitch. She said I was also speaking in a peculiar dialect she's never heard before.

As she entered the room, she saw me rocking back and forth, with hands and arms crossed in front, still speaking in the same undetectable language. Instinctively, she said she grabbed the chair I was sitting on, and began to shake it and me, trying to break whatever state I was in.

Over the years, my mother and I have concluded the strange dialect I was speaking was actually the blessed gift of tongues.

How did a young child such as Holly, express benedictions through such a sacred dialogue? What drove her living spirit to such a place where it could remember ancient idiom?

Holly's mother said her daughter also seemed to be calling out to someone during the ordeal. Was she summonsing the angels? Were the small lights surrounding the dark shadows really warriors from heaven? I sincerely believe the memory, which Holly described, was the scene of an unearthly battle, a conflict between demons and celestial soldiers.

Of course, this example of angelic battle is on the verge of the extreme, but one that was so severe, it penetrated our world with undisputed power. Allow me to retract. It makes easy sense for God to keep His angels near rather than far and away. There must be some form of a guard ship over mankind; to keep the gates of hell sealed; and the gates of heaven wide open.

Holly was part of the conscious and sub consciousness of two worlds colliding. As individuals we all have moments of awareness of celestial presence in our lives. But out of fear or ignorance we choose to forget or deny those moments.

Spiritual awareness in children is much stronger then adults. Why? In this a subconscious decision, to forget the knowledge given to us at birth and become spiritually closed as adults?

As humans we have the ability to consciously choose to block out existence of the Devine in the physical sense, but isn't it easier to think of heavenly grace in the form of religious devotion and church, rather than physical bodies of energy in our personal surroundings?

A few examples: When we meet a complete stranger who is willing to give whatever is necessary, to service another's need, is that an act of Devine intervention, or nothing more than a good

Samaritan at work; when a white feather falls from the ceiling of a church during service, did it fall from a celestial wing or merely a molting bird dweller taken up residence in the rafters; and when we see a ball of twinkling light floating at our side, is it an angel or just a sign of fatigue?

We, as humans, know what we are sensing, but have lost the freedom of the free spirit that acknowledges those senses. Religion and its formality come from learning to worship by the rites; bringing many restrictions to the knowledge we have been given, way before learning the regulations of doctrine. We may have, in our personal journeys in order to find Higher Power, lost the knowledge of the true spirit.

Angels have always been angels, and were nothing else before. They have been the same rank and stature in heaven, in-between, and even on earth. They are a loving and emotional race of beings that adore and love humankind, as they do one another. Their mission on earth is under God's direction to serve us with their heavenly memory still intact.

Visitations from celestial beings are a true blessing and physical proof of God's great hierarchy. A special emissary must at very just times, send messages of personal information to us, and only His angels could only carry such herald of intense holiness.

Almost all life-after-death experiences involve the sighting of a celestial. Time and time again, individuals say they are being lead into a bright, glowing light, by an image of a winged creature. I have to admit; I am one of the same, who has experienced the same type of intense holy vision.

During the summer months of 1997, I discovered a small lump at the side of my throat, just underneath my jaw. I was the mother of small children and shrugged off my extreme tiredness with that same foundation. My health began to decline and I was quickly turning from fair to poor condition. I decided to make an appointment to see the doctor to investigate the strange lump on my neck. Surprisingly, the doctor only ordered a few blood tests. When those tests came back normal, her only advice for me was to just watch 'it,' and if 'it' changed in any way, give her a call.

I, in turn, opted for a second opinion as was referred to a specialist. He said it might be just a goiter. He ordered several different tests, assuring me that at my age (30, at the time) the chances of cancer were very unlikely.

During this time of physical turmoil, my husband was going through a job transfer, taking us back to Bisbee. I decided to wait for a diagnosis, from a doctor there instead.

Regardless of what I was thinking, my health began to plummet. I was incredibly tired, my appetite poor, my color was ashy, and I developed very dark circles under my eyes. I simply felt terrible.

During that period I was stressed over moving and compounded by the fear of being struck with cancer, a disease that I was genetically set up for. This was the same illness that took so many of my family members, from my grandparents, cousins, aunts and uncles, and my mother, all victims of the same tortuous blight.

At the time, of my celestial experience, my husband was working the graveyard shift. One evening, as I lay in bed alone, I prayed harder than I ever had before; for the safety of my family, and to be well, for the sake of my children.

When I finally fell asleep, I only was to be awoken by a howling dog in the distance. I sat up in the dark and looked over to the digital alarm clock sitting on my nightstand. Many hours had passed. The clock read exactly three o'clock in the morning. I lied back, feeling suddenly strange, as if something was making its way toward me. Just as I was about to close my eyes, an overpowering compulsion guided my attention to my left and above the doorway and there 'She' was. My angel, in full glory, levitating above the doorway and looking straight at me!

Her golden brown hair was flowing over her shoulders in long, wavy, tresses; her ankle length gown, crisp and extremely white; and her dark eyes were barely visible, obscured by the brilliant orange-golden glow that was emulating from her statuesque figure.

Time seemed to stand still when I finally realized she was communicating without speaking, telling me to listen to the 'other' angel in the room, and take her hand. Turning from the apparition, I became aware of a second smaller angel to my right, evidenced only by the slight breeze fanning my hair. I couldn't actually see her but immediately felt my body being pulled upward, while experiencing a sense that I was flying.

I could feel the air currents below and above me, as we traveled, talking as we went along. We began to slow our pace as we entered a completely white environment. The deeper we penetrated the fogyish light, the broader my smile became, as the ambiance of peacefulness and pure love completely surrounded me.

The gentle being asked me a question I can't quite remember, but do recall my own reply:

"Okay, but only if Brittany and Chelsie will be all right," I said.

Then, and only then, did I realize what the fear of God meant. I was dropped and fell for what seemed for days, before breaking the membrane back into 'our world.' An excruciating amount of pain sent my body into an electrifying state of shock.

Now, completely conscious, the pain I endured could only be compared to having an electric cord strung through my entire body, then having someone plug it into the wall!

I watched my own body, as it violently shook my queen-sized waterbed, listening to the water in the mattress jiggle in short, and sharp waves. I was trying to scream out loud, but to my avail, realized I couldn't move at all. All of my limbs and voice were suddenly paralyzed! It was horrific! I had no choice, but to wait it out.

Soon, the numbness in my arms and legs turned into tingling sensations. I regained muscle movement and sat up to face the doorway. I instinctively looked up, searching for my angel, but her heavenly body was gone, leaving me behind and terrified, in the dark.

I refuse to analyze my angelic encounter, giving you, the reader a chance to interpret the experience in your own personal way.

Later, when my family moved back to Bisbee as planned, I was indeed diagnosed with thyroid cancer and had to engage in one outpatient surgery to remove two infected lymph nodes; a major operation, to remove my thyroid gland, and three diseased tumors;

and the radical radiation/iodine treatment to send the nasty cancer into remission.

I didn't have another celestial experience during my thyroidesctomy, nor did I dream of angels during my three-day recovery in the hospital. But, my recollection of the holy guide was clear and at times, I could definitely feel her presence.

Curiously, angel figurines and art work were gifts in abundance from friends and family throughout my recovery. Was this coincidence or invisible support, using the gifts as evidence of their constant presence?

For me, the angels' replicas living in my room were like strums of musical notes of holy devotion. To listen too when my emotions were down and my fear was spreading into complete anxiety, lifting me through my illness. The positive energy of the angels worked with heavenly threads, weaving gentleness, warmth and comfort, covering my existence with the simplicities of life.

Perhaps the visit from my guardian angel was just a bit premature, since it was not my time yet, despite her urgency to save me. But angels do have imperfections (such as the members of the human race) and makes mistakes from time to time. They are sent to guide us to the best of their abilities, but sometimes, are blinded with emotional jargon resulting in poor judgments.

Angels fend off evil and demonic spirits while attempting to guide us in the right direction as messengers of God. The angels pray for the human soul and for its needs, as well as worrying about its ultimate outcome. At the time of death, angels are to guide the human spirit to paradise, but when my angel grew anxious for my new beginning in the afterlife, she accidentally fell out of the groove of my destined death. Instead she enlightened my sights to her kind's existence and strengthened my spirit to finish my true mission in life.

Angels glide on holy light, carried by God's aspirations for the human race. They don't live their existence with the anatomy we are used too, adorned with white, fluffy wings, etc. (Though, that is pretty much how I saw mine.) I accept as true, that they come in whatever form is necessary and will emerge in the figure of a woman or of man; a boy or have a girl; or even sometimes arriving in such a bizarre form, not able to configure.

Beware of demons disguising their wart-covered exterior complete with large gnashing teeth. Taking any form necessary to deceive and manipulate us humans into their puppets of evil deeds. Take heed; 'gut feelings' are important when an entity is attempting to confuse your spirit with questionable demands and cling to the power God gave you before entering this world.

Call in all the heavenly information imprinted into your own soul's heart of legions, and what defines your holy loyalty. You were made a dyad with your guardian spirit an epochal before your day of birth. God gave careful plan to each and every soul on this planet, with delineative devise, suited for the completion of its mission and to pass it onto eternity. With this in mind, we should try to remember that the races of angels are His army, created to protect cruelties of the Devil himself, and to help us to the finish line of life, unscathed.

Taken from the True Catholic Website: *Eph. 2-19: Now therefore, ye are no more strangers and foreigners but FELLOW-CITIZENS WITH THE SAINTS, and of the household of God.*

Acts 12-7: And behold the angel of the Lord came upon him and a light shined in the prison; and he smote Peter on the side, and raised him up, saying: Arise up quickly. And his chains fell from his hands.

Heb. 1-1-14: Are they not all ministering spirits, set forth to minister for them who shall be heirs of salvation?

Luke 15-10: Likewise I say unto you, there is joy in the presence of the angels of God over on sinner that repenteth.

Feel free to call upon the angels for protection. They were created to serve and will arrive at the moment of being summoned. God is pleased when His angels are commanded, as are the holy creatures. Every morning and each night, I pray for God to bless and cover my family and friends with his blood and to send His 'golden angels' for holy protection from the evils of this world. I sincerely try to keep His angels close, while remembering we are all separate sectors of God's creation, and hold different powers from His glory.

Taken from the Website True Catholic: *Our guardian angels help us by praying for us, by protecting us from harm, and by inspiring us to do good.*

(Tobias 12:12) When thou didst pray with thy tears, and didst bury the dead, and didst leave thy dinner, and hide the dead by day in thy house, and bury them by night, I offered thy prayer to the Lord.

When people we are close to die, we want to think they somehow transform from human to angel. But to believe this, deprives His ostensible purpose for the human soul.

When we ultimately reach perpetuity, our soul does indeed configure into another bodily form, but not an angelic one. It is not ignorance to believe in the version of a loved one becoming an angel, if it soothes one during the time of mourning. A family may feel that their departed has spouted wings upon death, but; Angels have always been angels; such as humans have always been human.

Look upon His celestial army as a separate being, and having a different place in Heaven, and on earth. They are awesome defenders of the Word of God and of His human children.

When our time comes to crossover and finally rest in peace, the angels will continue to live in the same state of heavenly immortality and not metamorphosing into a different species, but staying in their destine grandeur. It is our individual decision to accept the glory of our Higher Power, and to permit the mightiness of His angels.

When we are at the end of our time on earth, we take the hand belonging to the so-called 'Angel of Death.' The angel that must be more gentle and amiable then what is described, as a creature dressed in a black cape, holding a large machete. A kinder, more peaceful being must be present to make the passage to heaven more pleasing.

Taken from the Website True Catholic: *Then shall the just stand with great constancy against those that have afflicted them and taken away their labors. These seeing it, shall be troubled with terrible fear, and shall be amazed at the suddenness of their unexpected salvation. (Wisdom 5:1-2)*

Such an example, was the atrocious scene played out on September 11, 2001. The morning of the angels: A day filled with terror, pain, and shock. After the first place hit the World Trade

Towers (WTC), God's army of angels were trumpeted to comfort the innocent passengers of the high-jacked planes, surrounding the buildings and direct the horrified men, women, and children, to their destiny. Pictures of people jumping out of the WTC towers imprinted my soul with their impeccable bravery. Over the next couple of years, I could still see the image of people falling from the skyscrapers; still shed tears at their bravery; and still be in awe of their seeming incredible calm.

One photo in particular has remained in my subconscious. It was a man jumping from a window of the first tower hit. The young man's freshly ironed, yellow shirt; his slicked back, light brown hair; his khaki pants were perfectly creased; and the dark brown Loafers he decided to wear to work that day, were all clear through the eye of the camera.

Also apparent in the camera's eye and most astonishing, was his composure. There were no wildly flaring arms, nor feet kicking in panic. Rather, his arms remaining at his side, head down, as if skydiving, without fear, confident.

What state were each of the victims in as they jumped to their death? Why did that man in the yellow shirt seem so serene, and where did they find the courage to jump?

I believe those who leapt to their death, saw something the rest of us could not. They were witnesses to an incredible display of holy intervention. The angels were summoned to guide those trapped by fireballs sent straight from hell, to save them from unbearable torture and pain. Surrendered those who leapt from the buildings that September morning, and were unconditionally giving themselves to God. Their demonstration of faith witnessed by billows around the world.

Chapter X

The human spirit has the ability to love and to hate, to feel remorse and to satisfy the urge of revenge. We live out individual destinies while choosing between the paths of good and evil. As innocent children, we are accepting to initial feelings before dissecting them with cynical aspirations, while living in blind faith.

During bedtime and during the time of my daughter's very young childhood, Brittany was presented with quite an honor by being greeted by beatific grace.

I had bought both girls individual statues of the Virgin Mary from a tiny, local gift shop. Chelsie's was a majestic music box, with the Virgin and Child turning in full circles as it played a traditional song devoted to the Mother of God. Brittany's was a statue/night light of the Virgin holding her hands in prayer.

The light was turned on every evening before the girl's were tucked in for the night, and the music box played as the children said their prayers. A special evening unfolded when the girls asked if the Virgin Mary was in the room when they said their prayers. I was very surprised when they asked me such a sweet and intuitive question.

"Yes. I believe she is here, with God, listening to your needs and wishes," I told them.

After moments of silence, with only the music box playing and the three of us looking at the night-light, the last 'good night' was finally said. Upon leaving the room and shutting off the light, I heard Brittany mumble words I could not understand. Then quite suddenly, she yelled out to me.

"Mom! Come here! Mom!" she screamed with excitement.

"What, silly…what?" I said, as I turned the light back on and reentered the room; Brittany was already sitting straight up, with eyes wide open.

"Mom, she said she loved me too!"

"Who did?"

"Virgin Mary!"

"What?" I said in amazement, as I looked over toward Chelsie who was also sitting up in her bed by now.

"Mom. When you turned off the light, I closed my eyes and said, 'I love you Virgin Mary.' I heard a woman's voice in this ear (motioning her small hand over her right ear). She said, 'I love you too.'"

"Oh Mommy!" whispered Chelsie.

"Wow! How amazing! See girls. She hears you when you talk to her. Let's tell her we love her too. She'll like that."

In unison, we did just that. I told the girls to lie back and try to go to sleep, since Brittany had the first day of second grade to attend and Chelsie was going to help me with the grocery shopping early the same morning.

I recently asked Brittany if she recalled the incident. Her response was, "Oh, my gosh! You remembered that! I remember! Her voice was right in my ear! That was cool."

It's amazing what can happen when a person is completely open to the forces of the true spirit. Innocence of a child is a blessed virtue. A characteristic usually lost when different interpretations of God's words are presented in various religions.

The pragmatist, afraid to realize his or her ability to love freely and limiting all possibilities of other dimensions fogs the chastity of 'openness'. Another strange and mesmerizing incident took place, ten years after the death of my mother, by someone who obviously had not lost her ability of blessed virtue.

When she died in 1992, I was devastated but still able to pray for her passage through the gates of heaven, to go with ease and leaving no regrets of leaving her children, was the one thing I could find the strength to do.

That happened when I was twenty-five, and many years have passed since her death, but on occasion, she visits me in my dreams. Her appearances in the dreams are identical to when she was alive.

Her body weight, length of hair, and personality seems the same before she got ill. Her presence in the dreams is strong, yet gentle. She never speaks, but is always sitting or standing at my side. There are no reasons for her visits, no drama, nor advice is ever given.

When I woke from the dreams my mother appeared in, I forgot for a second or two that she was deceased. Her presence was so strong that I believed she was still alive. Funny, when I realized I was just dreaming her, I wasn't extremely sad, just lonely.

I admit, I do miss her from time to time, but I have gotten used to being without a mother. Used to not the maternal advice of raising my children, or marriage counseling usually given to daughters. I really have become comfortable with being dependent upon myself when any sorts of problems arise in my life.

On a late fall evening, I received another type of message from my mother. She communicated with someone who was close to the family. A person whom she knew when she alive, but would not have possibly known that same individual was connected to me again, at present.

The phone rang at approximately twelve o'clock at night, waking me. I answered with a curious hello, and was surprised to hear the voice on the other side of the phone line. The woman was a good friend of one of my older sisters when they were teens, and whose parents were also close to mine. Now the individual is the mother of one of my child's close friends.

The family acquaintance began to apologize for calling at such a late hour, and then continued to tell me what had just conspired in her home. She said my mother; Mrs. Rojas had just spoken with her. Before I could respond, she assured me she wasn't crazy. I believed her as soon as it came out of her mouth. The woman continued to tell me that over the past two weeks, her own daughters informed her that they had the strong feeling of a woman's presence, and how they seemed to become more and more nervous as the days passed.

I told her, my mother had passed over, and how we occupied the house they were currently living in around the time of her death. I told her that was the last house she remembered us in, and how my husband Bill, used to prune the big pomegranate tree into the form of an umbrella, to give her shade when she would have cold drinks on hot, summer days.

The voice on the phone said that she and her daughter were watching a movie in the back room, when her child fell asleep. After watching the rest of the tape, the woman said she had the sudden urge to bless the picture of my daughter on the dresser beside the bed, before turning off the television and VCR.

At the moment of closing her eyes, she saw a very bright glow surrounding the room. Because of the illumination, she could easily see the decorations of butterflies hanging on the wall nearest to the bed. Then, she said she heard the voice of my dead mother. She said the spirit was hovering right over her and her daughter!

The family friend said couldn't see her, but she just knew some how, that it was actually she! The message to me was that she (my mother) knew I was going through rough times, and she was worried. She also told the woman to tell me she was sorry for what she did to me, and to please forgive her.

I hung onto every word and every sentence. Amazed and very confused. How and why did she come back from passing over? From the description of her visitation, she seemed to be in the state of Glory. What would have caused her to come back, after all of these years? Why now?

The family friend continued to tell me that my mother's spirit just kept repeating herself over and over. She told her, "Mrs. Rojas, she's all right and that she should just go back home." She said the glow she brought with her was so bright, but didn't frighten her. Her presence wasn't bad.

The following day I went to my mother's gravesite and prayed for her soul's peace. I pleaded for God to watch over my mother and to tell her I would be all right. That I would forgive whatever she felt guilty of and that she must return home.

I don't know how it works, when a person dies and goes to God, then receives some sort of permission to return. Why, and especially how did my mother's spirit return to this earthly realm? This strange incident opened my mind to several questions: When a person passes over, do they actually go directly to God? Is there another place to be before returning home? A place of consciousness putting you through more tests and situations of how you would use the gift of your free will; If you didn't live morally, do you get a second change in this 'other' place, to recover your right into heaven? Is this what happened to my own mother? On what grounds was her 'returning' permissible? For what purpose was the visitation made? Was this her second chance? Maybe, but I really don't know what exactly made her feel so bad or guilty. She loved her children and did her motherly duties while raising my brothers, sisters, and myself. I can't really think of the real reason for her return. That's between her and God I suppose. I hoped, for whatever reason, it helped her through an unexplainable and complex situation.

The path to righteousness is hard, but a very pleasant thing to remember is— it is never ventured alone. We have our assigned spirit guides, angels, and have course, God to help direct us in the right way. Through prayer, we may ask for another's well being, hoping for even more 'help' then what is already available to us every day.

As mentioned before, I do the very thing several times a day for family, friends, and enemies, blessing and wishing for strong, spiritual healing and protection. During another time when I was experiencing great, personal turmoil, I had the urge to go to St. Patrick's church, so on a weekday and early afternoon, I chose to drive from my house to lower Tombstone Canyon, since I usually walked the approximate one and a half mile distance from my house.

My heart was heavy and my body tense with stress. I have lived the majority of my adult life relying on self for solving personal dilemmas, but this time I needed the help of another.

As I drove up the hill leading to the back parking lot of the church, I began to feel slightly less stressed. The tightness of my back muscles gradually relaxed, causing me to let out a long, deep breath as I put the car into park.

The walk from the car to the front entrance was very enjoyable.

The breeze was gentle and filled with the light scent of roses, from the bushes lined along the cement path, positioned along the side of the elaborate building. The sky was deep, clear blue and the sunshine surrounded my body with warmth.

I opened one of the wooden doors and slowly entered. Careful not to disturb anyone who might be in the church. As soon as my feet touched the floor of the entrance way, I looked around the majestic sanctuary and said, in a very low voice, "Hello..."

I went directly to one of the marble containers filled with holy water and made the sign of the cross, then began to walk toward the altar. All of the pews were empty, making it very easy to pick one at the very front, to begin my praying. As I put my car keys on the wooden bench, I made a face cringe as I reacted to the echo of the metal hitting the hard surface. I then pulled the kneeling bench down and positioned myself for comfort. Before adjusting my hands in a praying position, I looked up at the life-sized statue of God placed at the top of an incredible altar, replicated like an elegant and detailed white, castled basilicas.

Without taking my eyes off the blessed statue, I began to pray out loud. This was the first time in my life that I spoke out loud to God in this, or any other church.

My praying was not in the usual fashion, but with a collection of deep-seated questions of why my life was where it was, at that time. My tone was not angry, nor sarcastic, but rather very emotionally straight forth. As I continued to ask God why, my eyes bared witness to an awe-inspiring moment in time.

The same type of orange-yellow glow I saw my angel appear with, began to emulate from behind the statue's head and shoulders! The color of the light was much deeper and brighter than the celestial's, forcing my eyes to water. As the glow intensified, the ceramic figure's face began to materialize into human flesh!

I began to softly cry and rubbed both eyes in disbelief. I don't know how, but I continued to talk in perfect dialect, staring at the incredible sight, in shock.

The face was now covered with real-looking hair. His beard dark and on his long, wide nose, a small lump appeared on its bridge.

His eyes…I can't even begin to find the words to describe how they penetrated straight through my body and soul! He didn't utter a word, or send a forewarn-filled message, but the force I experienced draped me with a feeling of complete protection and love.

The intense glow gradually faded out, and the previous state of the statue returned. I then turned my entire body around on the kneeling bench, and placed my head on the pew. I covered myself with my hands and arms and began to cry with little control.

When I finally regained my composure, I walked out of the church in a strange, meditative condition. Before I realized it, I had already driven halfway home!

I was filled with a type of happiness never experienced before. Ever. I remember thinking, "I thought if you saw the face of God, you would die." I looked at my hands on the steering wheel, at my arms, and at my breathing chest and said out loud, "Well, they must be wrong, 'cause I am definitely still alive."

That experience was the reassurance I needed, to get myself strong and confident. Ready to face the problems I had to deal with. God will do whatever is needed to help you and never at any point, will leave your side.

My own father, several years ago, told me about the same type of grace bestowing upon him and my mother during their short-lived time in Hollywood, California.

Upon an evening walk down the strip, they passed some sort of gospel church. The singing and clapping were extremely loud, and caught their attention as they strolled by the opened door of the building. Suddenly, my dad said my mother stopped and grabbed his hand and said she wanted to go inside. With very little coaxing, my father agreed.

He said the church was decorated with crosses, red carpet, and was very lit-up inside. They chose to sit in the very back and sat quietly, listening to the congregation praise God with song and dance.

Soon, a reverend began to speak atop the one-step-high, stage altar. My father said he spoke of God's love and strength, of God's glory and His hope for all mankind. Then, out of nowhere, my dad said my mother suddenly stood up and walked straight toward the black reverend.

My father said he tried to stop her but couldn't. What happened next was so amazing; he said he didn't think I'd believe him.

He said, "When your mom reached the stage, she stood facing the whole church and held her hands and arms wide-open. The reverend stood back and began to pray really loud! Then, Francine...your mom rose about six inches off the ground and floated from one side of the stage to the other! A little boy ran from his seat to your mother and held his little arms up and began to cry! I could see the tears just roll down his face. The whole church went crazy!"

I just couldn't embrace what my dad was saying, at first. I never saw him as a religious person, but from the expression on his face, as he told his story, convinced me he was telling the truth.

He continued his story, "That lasted for quite a few minutes before she simply floated back to the ground, then walked through the center isle, back to me. She sat down blank faced. I asked, 'Frances! Are you all right?' She answered me with a confused look and said, 'Why wouldn't I be?' She didn't remember a thing, Francine."

Sometimes I feel if an individual becomes too close to the understandings of God, if they tune in on the graces of His work, and somehow began to realize the meaning of His existence, they are 'taken' away. Those who seem overly spiritual and become unusually close to God, congruously die at their peak time of worshiping. Not always, but in my observation of that very subject, that is what usually happens.

I knew of two teenaged girls, who were both very involved in their churches and inordinately absorbed toward the deification of God's gospel. They enjoyed mostly social engagements associated with their parishes. Dances, shows and plays, and of course the activity of their church youth's organizations.

These young women were very honest, innocent, and giving people and enjoyed the learning of scripture and the interpretation of those holy words, while becoming very intuitive of God and his plan for all mankind. Their devotions to those plans were their own personal journeys of righteousness for all to follow, seemed overwhelmingly developed for such young women. But, by doing such an exceptional job of spreading and living God's word may have earned the honor of sitting at His side, assisting with bigger and more complex missions. They both died at the ages of 16 and 17, as my mother died about two years after the phenomenon played out at the Hollywood church, soon after her peak of gospel redemption.

I am not saying, "If you get too close to God you will die." What I am trying to make known, is my theory of God's recognition for an individual whose loyalty is way beyond the normal degree of earthly spirits, but acceptable for the prompt delivery to Grace.

A soul so pure and filled with 'blind faith,' that it is apparent to heaven's council, that a long and sometimes suffered life is unnecessary for the metamorphosing of living spirit to the ultimate state of Glory.

Cutting the lifetime of being continuously tested, to an easier transition from planet Earth to the plate setting at God's table. A place, which is reserved for all who chose to believe…

Chapter XI

My experience as a professional writer begins with a position at a local newspaper that terminated its circulation in the year of 2000. I will direct my point of interest to the building the business was housed in. The large structure is located in the Warren District of Bisbee, now transformed into a fitness club. The history of the structure includes a medical clinic and the site of a successful law practice.

I spent approximately three years at the newspaper. While there, discovered the presence of two entities that seemed quite comfortable in the working environment, stirring up turmoil when employees were left alone, working on deadlines, or the first to arrive for the day. The two energies in the building made scarce visits, and seemed quite passive.

I often heard the strange "shush" of two men talking in and around the building. Their voices were low and deep, and not actually whispering, but keeping their voices to a minimum. I didn't discuss the strange sounds, voices, or cold spots in the office with other staff members at first. I wanted to keep the knowledge, of these kindred spirits a secret not wanting to cause any sort of uneasiness among the troops.

Of course this way of thinking changed when an unusual E-mail was sent to the paper, asking for a reporter to accompany a paranormal investigating group on a Saturday afternoon in historic Bisbee. Of course, when my editor asked me if I wanted the assignment, I accepted the story with eager anticipation. Apparently the investigators received news of the legendary antiquity of Old Bisbee, recognizing this as a perfect place for an old fashion spook hunt.

Before the scheduled day of the inquisition of the alleged haunting in the momentous neighborhood, I decided it was time to tell my co-workers of the strange encounters in the office complex. Surprisingly, the staff had their own list of unusual experiences to discuss.

A graphic artist reported she often felt invisible caresses from an unseen caller. She noted the entity would gently rub her calf and at times *it* would stroke her hair. Incredibly, the woman never felt fearful since the phantasmal touches seemed gentle and kind.

A columnist for the paper confided in me and told me of her own odd encounters. She said the same as the graphic artists. They occurred when no one was around. While concentrating deeply on a piece, the writer said she often felt the urge to turn around and see who was standing behind her. Every time that happened, no one was there. Once in a while, she said she viewed a shadow toward her back reflecting on her computer monitor. As soon as she turned completely about face, the figure always vanished.

When I brought up the low tone of voices I heard in the building, she abruptly responded with, "Get outta here! When I come in the morning, no one is usually here yet. I hear a number of voices whisperings all around this place. It's really creepy."

The usual were evident with other staff members, encounters of strange origin would only happen when they were by themselves. Another writer told me she would see blurs of someone walking into the front office area, as she worked late into the evening, alone. The seasoned journalist said she was never alarmed over her supernatural encounters, and chose to ignore the visions, returning to her work every time she saw one.

My experiences were different in the way of their severity. My meetings with the spirited energies were of a more aggressive nature. I often heard the sound of hard, heavy footsteps walking toward my work area. As they grew closer and closer to my desk, I would constantly feel a collectiveness of rage and frustration. The beings seemed angered that I was sharing the building with them, worried that I had the ability to uncover their surreptitious existence.

My ultra sensitivity of banshees in the office may have caused a paranoid notion of banishment, making the lost souls confused by picking up on my own energies and becomingly aware that they somehow didn't belong here. Realizing, they had died.

Often many changes were made at the paper. From rearranging office equipment, to new staff hires and frequent dismissals, nothing stayed the same. Change is precisely something an unearthly embodiment of a human soul dislikes. To alter the environment in any way will cause a poltergeist type reaction.

During the supernatural encounters, I recited impending prayers that may have clicked the doorknob of their entrance to 'the other side.' A place they have constantly tried to avoid, as they walk this earth with the constant denial of their own death. Conjuring a plan to stay in the strange dimension they keep themselves imprisoned in and the place where they veil their reality.

They also restrict themselves to the place where they were most happy, or the location of their most horrible demise. Whatever the reason for my unpopularity with the forces haunting the building, they explicated their feelings toward me very well.

I was very eager to share my stories with the paranormal experts from Phoenix, wanting their determinations of the facts unfolding in the workplace. The investigators were a collaboration consisting of several members, but only six made the trip to Bisbee that afternoon.

The newspapers' place of business was where the paranormal investigators began their search equipped with one digital camera, a video camera, and 35mm cameras (including my own), to capture the entities on film.

The group said they have caught several 'orbits' of energy (the easiest form a spirit may take, resembling a floating transparent round bubble) before, and was hoping to accomplish the same on that day.

I told them of the strange incidents, and where they usually occurred. The leader of the organization began to take pictures with her digital camera. She could not find anything peculiar, but the group was patient and continued for almost 45 minutes before something became evident.

"Over here in graphics, it's cold in here. The hair on the back of my neck is standing up," said member number two.

The photographer using the digital camera walked over to the office and began to take several pictures, turning up nothing. She immediately walked down the hallway and began to take a few more pictures.

"I see something…" called the picture taker.

We all crowded around her and saw two orbits in her camera's viewfinder. One was floating low to the ground, and the other was floating in the middle of a hallway.

"Sometimes we have to call them out, so they can feel comfortable enough to present themselves," said a male member of the group.

Content with those visions, we all decide to go on to our next stop, which was Hotel La More/The Bisbee Inn, a 24-room, hotel building built by S.P. Bedford in 1916, on two lots, located on "OK Train," now OK Street, on a site where two residences were previously destroyed by fire. Bedford furnished the hotel and leased it to Kate La More on Oct. 1, 1917, according to literature available at the Inn.

The Hotel sits on a very narrow and steep hill, directly above Brewery Gulch. As I walked behind the paranormal investigators to the designated site, I took notice to the energies from the past, rise from the Gulch. As I took each step, faint flashes of the pusillanimous souls of the days of old, showed me how it used to be…

We all reached the staircase leading from the back street of Brewery Gulch to the top of OK Street. The steps are made of rusted old metal, but still solid.

Since I was the first to reach the top, I looked back down at the incredible view of the entire neighborhood. It was a breathtaking moment. The flow of the landscape was antique, but suddenly very new. I was swept into the warm breeze that blew back the collars of my light jacket, sensing all that had passed below me.

My husband Bill carried my camera bag (he decided to come along, due to his substantial curiosity) and as he reached the top, asked if I was all right.

"What? Yes, I'm fine. Let's go." I replied.

As I crossed the narrow street to the entrance of the Inn, my eyes focused on the crafted beauty of the building. The efforts to keep the structure in its original splendor may have been too successful, causing lost souls of the past, ambiguous to the actual time era of present day. Adding another explanation why the entities may still dwell here, and at other sites of historical Bisbee.

As we finally entered the establishment, the ambience of the structure definitely reflected upon its era. The front doors are made of dark, heavy wood and the staircase leading from the entrance to the main floor, all mirror the elegance of the distinguished building.

As I climbed the stairway, the surroundings seemed to pull me backward into time, as I ironically walked forward.

The General Manager, a charming middle-aged woman, greeted us with alluring interest. She made it around the gorgeous receptionist counter, (made of the identical material as the entrance) and put her hand out to shake that belonging to the leader of the investigators. Another member videotaped the General Manager as she told of the paranormal activities at the bed and breakfast establishment:

"After so many guests reported strange experiences, we asked them to log them for us. One saw a woman float down one of the stairways, another said she could smell lilac water in her room. Our housekeepers have said that on several occasions after making up a bed and leaving the room, they returned to find it messed up again," said the executive.

She said the second floor seems to be the most active, especially rooms 14, 15, 16, and 17.

"Room 15 has reports of an imprint of a body on the bed in the room and when a person is in that bed, they said they can sometimes feel the weight of someone sitting on the bed."

After the short presentation of alleged haunting made by the manager, I instinctively made it to Room 15. I stood at the doorway of the empty room, as 'check out' time had just passed, leaving the Inn primarily vacant and a perfect time for the investigators to take a closer look of each area of sightings.

With camera in hand, I took pictures of the bed that the administrator spoke of. The room itself is fairly small, and the white, rod-ironed bed sits in the middle of the area and is covered with a modestly colored quilt, adorned with several pillows. Directly in front of the bed, just feet from the foot rail, a full-running washbasin is positioned. The sink is decorated with a large wooden back with a medium sized, wooden framed mirror positioned directly above it. An antique appeal, a nice presentation repeated throughout the entire hotel.

The walls are adorned in an old-fashioned style paper. Patterns of diamond design connect on all four sides, in the shade of baby blue. A simple, white-laced curtain covers the one window, allowing rays of sunshine onto the bed.

As I carefully scanned the room, I silently called out to the infamous entity, "Are you here now? Do you want to take a sit with me?" I whispered.

I took a tempting chance and sat at the edge of the bed. I waited for an answer from the phantom. I closed my eyes, took in a long and calming breath, hoping to connect with the spirit. In a calm and slow manner, the hair on my body began to rise, as well as my heart rate, as the vibration of footsteps began to approach my location.

"Come, it's all right. I want to talk to you," I quietly said in just above a whisper. "—So, this is the home of the brave spirit huh?" With great disappointment, an older member of the paranormal group interrupted me, as he proceeded to enter the room.

I sat up and went to the doorway of the room and asked the man if he wanted to have his picture taken. He accepted the offer and posed at the end of the bed and put his hands on the foot rail.

The entire group of claimed psychics inspected the rooms where the haunting allegedly occurred, and expressed the most interest in the hallway of the floor more than anywhere else. The leader of the group began to photograph and was successful in seizing the entities with her digital camera.

That particular floor was occupied with two orbs hovering close to the ceiling, with one higher than the other. It seemed the spiritual beings were observing us from the elevated position and listening intensely for any information regarding their existence. Maybe they were also waiting for details of the whereabouts of their own families, since the hotel was made for travelers and visitors of the pioneers' populace.

Now that the banshees have been deceased for many years, talk of their passing among the paranormal investigators ignited a volatile amount of curiosity from their false reality. The questions of whom and why they are still residing in the hotel aroused their own suspicions. For a few moments, the curious notions of the investigating group pushed truth onto the entities, exposing their denial of passing on and coming to grips with their actual condition, which of course, was their own death.

We continued to investigate other areas of the hotel. We walked in a single file throughout the elegant dinning room. The eatery was placed in the center of the hotel and yet another area of special interest for the group. This is where the apparition of the floating woman was sighted, but sadly not on this day.

That was the last diligent try in that hotel. We decided to go to the next place of paranormal enquiry, the historical Copper Queen Hotel.

The Copper Queen Mining Co. built the hotel, shortly after the turn-of-the-century. The building is said to have been a proliferation spot for politicians, mining officials, and rovers. The Copper Queen Hotel is still a very popular site, with the reputation of hosting various celebrities, world-renown artists, and present-day bureaucrats.

The prominent structure also sits on a steep hill, such as most buildings in Bisbee do. The hotel can be seen from Main Street, and is positioned directly behind the Bisbee Mining and Historical Museum. To reach the hotel from Hotel La More, we had to back track our steps down the same steep, steel, stairway past Gore Park, and across to Howell Avenue.

The avenue is a tight, narrowed, street that inclines right off the bat and at a high angle. It is a one-way street that is also home to the

Y.W.C.A., the Covenant Presbyterian Church, and near the end of the road, is the site of Central School.

The Copper Queen Hotel is very close to the entrance from the Gulch. It is also the neighbor to a gourmet restaurant. As you take your first step onto Howell Avenue, the Grassy Park is to your immediate left. The park is one of the community's recreation areas as well as the landscape for the museum.

As we neared the graceful hotel, we passed several groups of tourists. One of the members of my group said, "Boy, this place sure is popular." Another mentioned how intriguing the hotel was as she climbed the wide, green-carpeted set of entrance stairs leading to the exquisite and swanky doorway.

On top of the steps and on either side is a covered patio. The areas are meant for dining a la fresco during mealtime or to enjoy a cocktail in front of the hotel's saloon.

The Copper Queen was very busy during the time of our arrival. As we entered the lobby of the hotel, a large crowd of guests was walking in and out of the double-door entryway. Tourists were bustling up and down the railed stairway, across from the lunch buffet, which was set up in the hallway, outside the bar area.

The leader of the paranormal congregate, approached the clear-glassed registry area and asked the in-keeper if the general manager of the hotel was in. As the hotelier called the manager on the phone, the rest of my group began to scan the southwestern artifacts decorating the lobby. Oddly, I focused my attention on the antiquated carpet of the area instead.

The flowers in the red rug were very enchanting to me. It reminded me of my Grandmother's kitchen throw down, in her Brewery Gulch home. The comparing designs triggered a flash into a strange moment in time and to an instant of another person's life and a long time ago.

As I stared at the carpet, I felt heat around my chest. I became instantly terrified with the feeling of someone chasing me down a hall, in the same building. In the vision, the hotel looked a little different then it did now. Women were in long dresses and adorned in big, fancy hats. I could smell the sweet mixture of tobacco smoke and light perfumes. The bustle of people was almost identical to the one on the present day. One distinctive observation was becoming clearer. My view was of a small child's perspective.

I felt myself running up the staircase to a higher floor, tripping on my own feet and busting my lip on the last step. Without hesitation, I continued to run down a long hallway, screaming and wailing out loud. The thunderous sounds of doors slamming shut were on both sides of me as I hurried down the corridor.

I could hear myself breath in uncontrollable pants. I could see the tears fall onto my tiny hand as it turned the doorknob to a room. As soon as I entered the chamber, I felt a hard shove to my back. The force threw my tiny body onto the floor. The sharp pain of bony hands wrapped around my waist, made me scream a bloody curl that echoed throughout the entire room! Then suddenly my vision became blurred, as if I was under water…

"Hello. I'll be right with you. Please go into the hotel's bar area. I am on the way to find the VCR tape of a recent television interview involving the various reported haunting here," announced the hotel's manager.

This sudden burst of information, given by this hotel's general manager, broke my trance and forced me to focus on my surroundings. After viewing a short documentation on the saloon's television, the hotel manager gave us a tour of where the most paranormal activities had been disclosed.

"The hotel is home to three claimed spirits. A male who appears to be in his 80s, a stripper named Julia Lowell, in her 50s (a room is named after her with a wooden nameplate reading, "The Julia Lowell Room"), and a five-year-old boy, who is said to have been drowned by his mother," said the administrator.

"Oh my God…the little boy…he was drowned. The blurry vision…" I thought to myself as the manager began to walk us up the staircase of the lobby. I stared at the floor of the steps and began to feel queasy.

The investigators photographed a large floating orb on the third floor, where the man has been sighted several times. Another orb was also visible in the digital picture, but floating much lower than the other, at just the right height for a small child.

After viewing the pictures, one of the more 'sensitive' members walked directly to the wall and put his right hand on the surface, feeling for the free energy captured on the digital camera. He brushed his fingers and palm from left to right, in a half-hemisphere motion, talking to the entities as he searched for their raw dynamism. After he turned away from the wall, he only took in a deep breath and said nothing.

The hotel's manager said that a guest on the fifth floor had once awakened at 3:15 a.m., to a woman dressed in black. She began to remove her clothing and when the man tried to reach out and touch her, she faded away.

"We have had several reports of different experiences by hotel guests. Two years ago at Thanksgiving time, a table of eight was enjoying a holiday meal in the dining room, when a little girl from the group continued to say she had to stay under the table, because she wanted to play with the little boy. None of the adults could see the entity," said the hotel executive.

Besides the popularity of the hotel rooms, the business also runs the well-received pub. It houses a beautiful, original wooden bar and along its north wall is a huge painting of a pudgy woman, lying on her side. The mood in there seems to be very pleasant and calm, while still holding the environment of spirited cheer, kept unscathed from its prime during the Wild West days.

My group inspected the lounge, but came up with nothing. We continued our tour of the hotel with the "John Wayne Room," named after the silver screen, superstar. This was a dwelling for the actor while he was on location in Arizona.

The walls of his room were completely covered with dark red roses, arranged in neat rows, in between thick maroon-colored stripes, from ceiling to floor. The windows dressed with matching mauve drapes and white lace curtains. An antique dresser and oval mirror sits in the far right corner of the majestic bed. What drew that

Hollywood cowboy to this particular hotel, legends of a different kind?

After several pictures were taken of the room, and when nothing unusual appeared in any of them, the manager took us to the top floor of the Copper Queen, where he showed us the machinery responsible for the working elevator. The same transportation systems where many guests have reported to see the elderly man appear then disappear on many occasions.

On the way up to the elevators motor room, the manager jested the men of the group to watch out for "Julia." He said she has the reputation for touching men who are visiting the establishment. Nothing of the sort happened, though if it did, it would have been a nice piece of entertainment.

Members of the group took more pictures, but alas, nothing out of the normal was recorded.

"Spirits have non-active days and are hard to track during those times. We may come back to the Copper Queen Hotel at another time," said the head of the researchers.

Why did the entities haunting the hotel choose to be quiet, except the little boy? He managed to tune into my own supernatural sensitivity and was successful in telling me the shocking account of his own death.

He found a way to flash me the horrific condition of terror he was in, as his mother chased him through the hotel, and the suffering he endured as she held him under the freezing tub water, as she gripped her hands around his tiny neck.

He let me hear the vociferating sounds of his mother's cursing words heard every time he managed to bring his head to the surface, only to be pushed back into the frigid water.

He let me feel the sensation of his blood rushing hot through his tiny veins as he struggled for his life.

He showed me the many colors of the tiny square tiles surrounding the tub, and the very bright light of the swinging light bulb above the two of them. The only objects he can remember focusing on, in between his violent dunking, and before his last breaths.

Finally, all he could feel was the exploding pain on the right side of his forehead. She had apparently, with one hand, pounded his head onto the floor of the tub, causing a deep lesion on the boy's head, causing his fatal injury, and his cruel death.

Despite the way the murderous scene of the child's death was shown to me, I still felt the overpowering of his love for his mother. Even after his own parent had taken his life so callously, he still held sincere feelings for her. He had forgiven her, but was confused to the fact, she was not here with him and he was alone. This type of malicious fatality may be the most sad and powerful kind of intense energy explosion ever imagined.

Next, on the list for the paranormal investigators was the Oliver House, a bed and breakfast located up the street from the Copper Queen Hotel. The B & B is nestled in a crevice of hills within walking distance of Bisbee's downtown. The building itself had been a man's dormitory during the depression era.

When we first arrived, we learned the manager was not available for a personal tour. The on duty shift cook and housekeeper volunteered any information she knew, but asked us to wait on the front porch of the Oliver House.

Quite frankly, I was becoming tired, both physically and spiritually. The connection with the child spirit at the previous hotel drained a lot out of me, making me feel placid and weak.

I took a seat on a piece of lawn furniture set out on the huge porch. This area of the old building faces a gorgeous view of the surrounding neighborhood. From the porch you can see the glorious mountains connected to the famed 'Glory Hole.' According to Bisbee historians, this at one time was also called the "Copper Queen Cut." This is the historical spot where ore was first taken from the new claims of the early community.

The gracious trees that surround Oliver House are pleasantly inviting and warming to the lucky individual enough to be resting on the veranda. I began to relax and watched the branches of the trees lining the yard wave gently in the wind. I watched the white-winged-doves pick tiny insects from the ground under the shade of the same trees, thinking to myself, "I could take a nap right now…"

The entire group was unusually quiet. I looked at everyone wondering if they had their own private connection with any of the entities we encountered in any of the sites we just visited. Or were we all stifled because we had one main point of a common gift, the ability to predict pandemonium.

My sedative state of serene was slowly uplifting to uneasiness. I began to now feel uncomfortable and felt a magnetic energy standing at one of the front windows of the B & B. I turned around and saw the curtains of the window move.

"What time is it? Does anyone know?" I asked the group.

"It is just after twelve," stated an investigator.

"So, do you think all of the guests have checked out by now?" I asked.

Before anyone had a chance to answer my question, we all turned our heads to the loud screeching sound of the front screen door opening. The House's cook said she was ready to talk to us now.

"Ma'am, have all the guests checked out yet?" I asked as I walked past her as she held the door open for the entire group.

"Oh yeah, sweetie! No one is here except us."

As we followed the woman down the long hallway, I realized this place was going to be a bit more active then the rest. We were led into the bed and breakfast's large country style kitchen. I suppose this is where the woman was most comfortable. She began to tell us of the many violent murders committed in The Oliver House, decades ago.

The worker walked back out into the hallway and stood in front of the staircase leading upstairs. She said at the first landing of the stairs, a man was shot in the chest, over an owed debt.

"I really don't have detailed information for you guys, but you're more than welcome to walk throughout the building. Feel free to inspect all of the rooms. Like I said before, they're all empty," stated the cook.

As the members of the group announced they would go directly upstairs to investigate, the kitchen door, which was held open by a worn, wooden, doorstopper, suddenly slammed shut! Almost simultaneously, the investigators began to photograph the door, emulating Hollywood paparazzi.

There was no apparent evidence of any stream of draft capable of pushing or sucking the door, a golden-brown color with thick wood, and with a large paned window, shut.

Moments passed before a few members of the group began to call out to the possible entity or entities responsible for the slamming door. A woman of the group walked over to the door and slowly opened it. As she made a closer investigation, I took a picture of her.

I thought I caught a glimpse of a phantasmal figure standing directly behind the woman. The figure mirroring a tall man with a slender frame was glaring at her, as she ran her hands all over the door. The weird silhouette in the glass reflection gave some solution to the mystery of the whipping door.

After that occurrence, we decided to move on. We all headed up to the second floor and inspected each room, one-by-one. As we reached the 'Cameo Room,' I and another member of the congregate felt negative vibes. I sensed an agitated presence, as the other person said he just didn't like the feeling he was receiving from that room.

The mentor of the paranormal investigating assembly, immediately entered the same room and instantly said she felt a tingling sensation.

"When I feel like that, I suspect a death by disease," she said.

The two paranormal experts began to call out to the entities, asking if it had died of a miner's disease. After the lead-woman photographed a small orb in the corner of the room, the weird impressions began to cease. A digital picture was taken of the exact area where I claimed to feel the most energy. A small orb was recorded there.

Did our own presence irritate that particular embodiment? Was it yet another lost soul able to hear our questions of 'why are *they* still here?' Implying they have already passed on and no longer live in the physical sense.

If the entity was listening to our voices, did it begin the process of pulling itself out of the spectral state? Was it agitated to the facts of its own departure of earthly life and its own stubbornness to leave the place of its life's demise?

As we walked out of the 'Cameo Room' I hard faint noises coming from another empty quarter. The sounds were replicating the sound of splashing water. I followed the noise into a room decorated in various shades of green. Under a small window, a wooden shelf held a hand painted, ceramic, washing bowl and pitcher. The sounds of an invisible washer faded away, but the impression of another was still evident.

I turned toward the hall where at the same time; pictures were being shot of my husband and an older member of the investigators, sitting on a couch at the end of the hallway. Later they confessed they were discussing the military. In the photograph, several orbits were sighted surrounding the two.

"They said this building used to be a man's dormitory. Maybe, the spirits were soldiers at one time or another," said a party of the group.

The feelings I received from The Oliver House, was mostly of severe loneliness and depression. The building reeks of male presences. The infamous gambling debts, owed to the frustrated men staying here may have caused murderous acts and a ripple effect of increased negative energy, which seems to permeate throughout the building. Broken love affairs, hard times and bad luck forced these particular men of the past to live here.

When the two men conversed casually on the couch, using their deep, keyed, voices they unknowingly attracted the banshees. The spirits stood around the men, hanging on every word, becoming completely involved in the discussion. Pulling energy from the memories of the living men, and strengthening their own vigor for staying in this place, they call home.

A masculine sense of pride was gloating at the end of the hallway in more forms then one. With my husband dressed in his cowboy's hat, and the other gentlemen's demeanor of an elder, it was very clear they were welcomed by the lost souls of The Oliver House.

We set on our way toward the next destination of paranormal investigation, The Bisbee Grand Hotel, located on Main Street. This building is very elegant, and is known as a popular social gathering place for locals as well as with tourists.

As you enter the hotel through the main entrance, the first thing that catches your eye is the luxuriousness of the carpeted staircase leading up to the hotel rooms. As you near the top of the steps, you will catch sight of a quaint table with matching chairs on each side. A gorgeous banister surrounds the opening to the floor. As you turn around to view the entire area, a gigantic skylight permits the bright Arizona sunlight to vibrantly shine over the entire entrance area.

The wallpaper is patterned in deep, red flowers, arranged in tightly bound bouquets. On the opposite site of the table and chairs, and behind the wooden handrail, French doors invite guests to a white, rod-ironed, fenced balcony. Directly above the double doors, a mosaic of Tiffany glass adorns the space in the same style of aristocracy décor. This old-style gleam throughout the hotel, as it keeps the building in fitting historic condition.

The leading member of the group said the manager of the Grand Hotel could not make a guided tour, but gave full permission for our group to look around. Each room has a different color theme and is decorated in elaborate adornments.

As members of the group wondered in and out of empty rooms, I chose to enter Room 2. Here I felt the presence of a man, but had a stronger sense of some twenties to thirties aged woman. I said a 'lady' not a prostitute. Something 'she' made sure I understood.

In another room, a set of child spirits was imprinted, around the ages of five and six years of age. Their giggles were heard, as they happily played alone and unattended by a mother or father. In the same second floor lobby, the energy of a long time attendant was felt. The entity travels from the staircase, around the banister and heads toward the outside balcony. A constant piece of memory tape repeated over and over.

Back in Room 2, an orb was photographed, but none others were recorded elsewhere. This hotel didn't feel heavily inhibited with negative supernatural flow, making this place a harmonious medium.

After we visited the Grand Hotel, we walked up the street to the Inn at Castle Rock. This establishment is located directly across the landmark entitled with same name. The Inn is one of the most fabulous structures in Bisbee.

The multilevel building sits directly above a twenty-something-foot-deep-ditch, making the erection very unique in its construction. The rock-mountain background streams right into the executive lobby for all to enjoy. It also houses the town's original water well, located in the middle of the dining area, now filled with Koi fish and a keen idea that works well with the Inn's guests.

This grand bed and breakfast is a fascinating and special architecture with eye-appealing attributes. Each space ranging from large too tiny is efficiently used as each room is embellished with different themes throughout the Inn. During the time of its construction, incredible blasting skill must have been used to form a space for building the huge structure.

In the back, besides the wondrous gray rock, an outrageous overgrown ivy-garden covers the entire landscape. Guests can follow a narrow trail up the hillside of the ivy area. The trail leads to a breathtaking gazebo made of golden stained wood. The very site of where a family-friend's beloved, pets' memorial was held.

The group was welcomed to investigate the numerous rooms of the Inn and only had the urge to photograph one site of interest, for paranormal purposes. An orb on a staircase leading to the private residence was recorded.

According to a friend of the proprietor, the father of the owner had died years before and was known to be very protective of his child...

Did we again unleash a presence? Was the gentleman still protecting his child after his death, giving reason why we didn't feel other energies in the Castle Rock Inn? He seems to be doing his job well and keeping his child safe from members of the other realm, succeeding in making this place a peaceful and tranquil environment.

That ended our touring expedition of paranormal activity in hotels of Old Bisbee. The paranormal investigating group said they make regular trips to continue their hunt of inexplicable experience around

Cochise County and other areas of Arizona.

When we all stood as one to call out the lost souls, 'they' had two choices; to turn toward the light of God; or to hide, making just of their own presences on earth. Some of the entities still residing in the historical hotels refused to make an appearance except the murdered child of the Copper Queen Hotel.

Maybe since he was killed during his childhood, his adoration for his insane mother blocked the sight of God's grace. His innocent thought of the only love he had experienced in his short life was that of maternal form. That tremendous power of loyalty forced this tiny soul to his damnation of becoming earthbound.

I truly enjoyed traveling about the historic establishments of my community with others who share the same type of curiosity and with the same gift of supernatural sensitivity. Which is the ability to feel the raw power of the human soul, after it has left its shell of flesh and bones.

When we are born into this world, we were given the disability of complete freedom. The will to feel and do, as we want as we walk through life, may be the most sincere and intense genre exhibited by God. Using His Grace as a peaceful transport to His kingdom is the only way to pass through the tunnel of light, and the only way to break through the membrane to eternal existence. God gave each living person ever born on this earth, the same exact liberty. It is the individual choice to use His gift with moral conduct and succeed in this life as well as in the 'afterlife.'

Chapter XII

The experiences that some paranormal psychics face throughout his life can bring a 'normal' person to their knees and can be sometimes miasmic. They can take every single bone of Christian faith to keep you from crossing into the other realm, as you fight the temptation to personally take the lost soul, back home yourself.

One who is sensitive to banshees, who walk this world, may in the beginning of discovery; feel alone, like an outcast. During the paranormal hunt performed in Historic Bisbee, I for the first time in my life, felt surrounded by individuals exactly like me. My personal experiences with the dead were harmonizing with others who have encountered the same type of events in their lives. These people, who I spent an entire afternoon with, verified my sanity. For when you live every day, consciously since childhood, with the supernatural whizzing around your head, you'd question your sanity as well. The paranormal investigators and I were a great force of power that helped to bring the entities out of their comatose state, for a few passing moments.

When the soul is in that state of confusion or denial, is when 'we' can feel their overbearing emotional crusade to stay earthbound, hallowing out their sense of reality, while bringing the living spirit to their immortalized existence to a complete halt.

The callings from the dead bear a high-propelled power of dismay and also bring high-pitched rings of tolling bells. Those sometimes-dark emotions can drape the living with eerie sensations of their existence. These special individuals may be a link, from this life to the 'afterlife', and a tie to memories of scenes of earthly life, whether they are good or bad, happy or sad.

To recognize the gift of psychic ability is not only a scary determination, when a person can see the cause of unexplainable incidents with strange clarity, he or she can begin to take steps to an incredible journey of insightful certainties.

The gift of supernatural sensitivity is a God given gift, and over time, becomes a developed craft of a more mature nature. This extrasensory skill can be artfully chiseled into the capability of recognizing deeply scarred souls that haunt land, buildings, and homes. Clarifying their insane reasons for staying earthbound and the ability to hear their cries from the other realm, we call death seems somewhat as an oxymoron of intrigue and fear.

The gift of sensitivity has its highs and lows. It can be a wondrous experience or a hell-like event that can scare the living daylights out of you. The experiences I have encountered have been both. The first entity, which came to me, was of course, the most endearing and revered in my memory. 'She' was luckily a purist of heart, wanting only to intertwine in my innocent spirit, and reveal in the memory of her own infant child.

The demure of the entity was quiet, yet strong enough to touch my living soul, with her sweet, maternal-like personality. This was the spark to the beginning of my psychic ability, a gentle push from the 'other side.'

Those lost souls, who choose to share their horrific deaths, are categorized as the hellish sectors of my terrifying supernatural experiences. The male presence I felt as a young child, the 5-year-old boy of the Copper Queen Hotel, and another child spirit, has been horrific incidents of spiritual capacity. The points of almost feeling the same types of terror exasperated by these lost souls have left me with emotional scars, lesions that have healed over time, but left remarkable marks on my own spiritual health.

The stains of a stranger's suffering have not damaged my inner light, but have only strengthen my faith in God and made my calling more clear: helping lost souls crossover to the other side and into the light, to find eternal peace.

I am not afraid, to stand strong in front of an entity crowding my personal space. I believe that when I tell a lost soul to go to God, I am not alone. His armies of angels are at either side, behind and before my earthly body and living spirit, ready to protect and defend God's word.

At times I choose to ignore the parade of souls that pass me by. I have shut out spirits that are dramatically captivated in their selfish demise. Those entities must be shut out, from time to time, to control the intake of the countless lost souls radioing in on my psychic energy. If I didn't do that once in a while, I would be a 'free-for-all' for the supernatural world.

I have learned how to channel the spirits before they have a chance, most of the time anyway. I try to 'see' them, before they 'see' me. This way, I have the upper hand, before they begin to draw my energy in, giving me the chance to figure out why they are denying their death and what may have generated such confusion and demented thinking.

The tools of the trade are faith and compassion for the dead, and for the living. These specific possessions of the true-spirit are vital to the compatibility of this realm and theirs. If we have complete faith in God's ways and feel for the departed with patience and understanding, then we will have the chance to show earthbound spirits to the light and to their glory.

These souls borrowing the flowing electricity from living bodies have to recognize they are wasting their time here. They must understand they have lived out their destiny and must move on. There is no time for suffrage when a spirit has fulfilled earthly duties and has come to the time of death, when all pain should end.

With the help of an individual's psychic skill, they may finally realize their true condition, and turn toward the bright glow of the eternal beam, leading the way to Glory and toward peace. When this ability is used in moral fashion, it can be an aide for the psychic and to lead toward his or her own destined triumph. At this time, the calling of God will be answered, to guide self and others who will follow the roads of genuine love, paved by Our Father, in this life, and the next, toward eternal bliss.

Such is the value of working as an instrument of God, is the worth of a supernatural sensitive, to be guided by the peace of all spirits.

Those who walk this world, as a bright and living entity, will thrive in an empowering face of truth. To live life as a free spirit and not letting anyone control their thoughts and ways of finding their own callings is a hard road to follow. A journey that one must endure to capture the essence of His grace, and a path that has to be traveled to truly enjoy life the way He wished it for you.

Chapter XIII

My most recent brush with the supernatural transpired at my residence in the Mule Mountains. An episode played out during the Christmas season and a period of time of communication with a child entity.

Approximately two years ago, after returning late at night with my husband of a night out, I checked on my girls and found them fast asleep in their bedroom, seemingly serene in their slumber. The next morning, Brittany told me the two of them had experienced something quite different.

She stated that the night before, she and Chelsie had immediately fallen asleep in their bedroom, after watching a movie on the television. A few minutes passed before she heard a strange noise she couldn't distinct, but then realized the banging noise was the rocking chair in my bedroom, hitting the wall every time it swayed back.

She woke Chelsie up and instructed her to grab a key chain with a picture of 'The Guardian Angel' from under her pillow. Chelsie instinctively held it tightly in her grip, as soon as she hurriedly followed her sister's orders. Ironically, this item was given to them by their Aunt Sally, just days before.

The racket continued for a while, until our Shih Tzu named Tootsie, began to bark at the chair. Brittany said Chelsie's cat, Precious began to meow and hiss, along with the snapping dog.

Suddenly, a loud "*Shussssh...*" was heard from an invisible intruder, with a tone of irritation geared toward the family pets. The girls were panicky and out of their minds at this point, feeling hopelessly defensive against the negative energy in the home. In desperation, they merely pulled the bed covers over their heads, hoping *it* would leave them alone.

Brittany said shortly after they heard the shushing noise, their room was filled with an incredible chill. She stated that the coldness swept over her head and body, before finally dissipating.

I was very angry. This damned soul, coming and disturbing my children when I wasn't around! After being informed of the eerie incident, I waited for *him* every evening, but he didn't come.

My husband would leave for work very early, leaving the three of us alone for a short period of time before everyone left the house for the day. I remember one particular morning, saying goodbye to him and falling rapidly back to sleep. I dreamt I was in a house with a pure and bright light shining through a bare window frame. I began to hear a loud and forceful crowd of both men and women parading down a hillside outside the structure. Their sounds were filled with anger and were fast approaching the house I was in. It felt as if we were high on a mountain and strangely enough, near the ocean.

Still inside the unfamiliar house, I saw myself running past all of the front windows, watching the strange mob march around and around the house. I saw a man with black, thick and curly hair at shoulder length, adoring a full beard yelling in a loud and low-pitched voice. He was screaming strange and vulgar chants, directing his speech toward the house. The crowd soon began to follow his lead, as they waved their tight fists over their heads…

"Buzz…buzz…buzz…" squawked my alarm clock, shaking me from the bizarre dream. I instantly remembered to wake my daughters for school, but before I could sit up from bed and open my eyes, I heard *him*. The entity that had dared to bother my unattended children, had finally decided to make an appearance, at last.

The reverberation of footsteps came from the left side of my bed, pounding on the hardwood floor, what sounded like hard-bottomed shoes. The gaits went right past my bed and onto the other side stopping at the antique, wooden, rocking chair positioned near my bed.

I still had not opened my eyes, nervous to see what was there. The temperature was freezing. I heard someone plop down on the wooden chair, then immediately began to rock back and forth in a quick fashion, hitting the wall with the back of the seat, every time!

Without hesitation, I decided to ignore the extremely negative energy sitting inches from my body, and called out to my daughters from the dark of the early morning light.

"Brittany! Chelsie! Get up!"

The strange and quick rocking continued, despite my voice. Then, suddenly I became angry. I turned my head toward the invisible rocker, and said, "Leave! You are not wanted here! I rebuke you! In the name of Jesus, I rebuke you! I am full of Christ, be gone! We are the living. You are the past. I command you to leave now!"

"Mom, what it is it?" cried out Brittany from her bedroom.

I could now hear Chelsie, now mumbling in the background. Without getting out of bed and moving from my position, I called back to the girls.

"Girls, pray with me now!"

In the most exquisite and powerful trio of harmony we began *Our Lord's Prayer,* each from our own beds.

"Our Father who art in heaven, hallowed be Thy name. Thy kingdom come. Thy will be done on earth as it is in heaven. Give this our daily bread. And forgive us our trespasses as we forgive those who trespass against us;...

The room was giving off a great deal of rancid energy. It felt like death.

"...and lead us not into temptation but deliver us from evil. Amen!"

I continued my words of deliverance. "You must leave now! You are not wanted here. I rebuke you in the name of Christ!"

I turned my concentration to my girls and said, "Brittany, get up. Turn your light on and come here. Chelsie, come here, now!"

The young girls came in my bedroom and sat at each of my sides. I turned on the small television sitting on my dresser and coincidently, a reverend was preaching of God's grace, on a televised church service. I turned back toward, the now motionless rocking chair, and said, "See, we are all Christians here, be gone now!"

The room was still cold and felt strange. I could feel the presence still sitting in the chair, and now next to Brittany. I held both of my daughters' hands and continued to pray.

"Please Lord, send your angels to protect my daughters and me from this presence. Lord, please save this, lost soul. It needs you and needs to understand it has passed!" I spoke directly to the spirit, "Go to Jesus, and go to Christ! Go home. Go with your parents and brothers, and sisters. Leave! You don't belong here. Let us be!"

Brittany calmly looked over at the empty rocking chair and said, "Mom, he has been here for a long time, he doesn't understand."

I looked at her with great surprise and said, "He has to understand! You know what, that's enough. You have to get ready for school, and I have to get ready for work. This is our home, not his. Go and get ready."

I got out of bed and stood right in front of the rocking chair. Picked it up and said, "My chair! Mine! Not yours, mine!"

I felt as if I had to speak in a direct and assertive way, as if I was talking to a child. I continued to ramble on about how the entity was in my house, and how this was my territory, and how he was now dead and didn't belong here with the living.

I set the chair down hard and took in a deep breath and blessed myself. I felt the entity move from the chair, but felt the energy still very much in the room. I decided to try to continue to get the morning back to normal as much as I could, and took a shower with the door open.

Approximately a half of an hour passed when Chelsie, already dressed, came up to me in the bathroom and said as she handed me a strange item, "Mom, look what Precious found. A cross."

The crucifix she gave to me was made from sort of cheap gold plastic replicating the Celtic Cross. I reached my hand out and took it from her tiny hand, instantly feeling the emotions of the sad, lonely emotions of the entity in our home.

"I've never seen this before. Where did the cat find it?" I asked.

"She had her paw under the oven, trying to get something, and I looked to see what she was after. Then I saw she was after this cross and pulled it out," replied Chelsie.

"Mom, that's a good sign. It's asking for help," stated Brittany as she stood behind her sister, standing on her tiptoes, trying to catch a glimpse of the strange item. She seemed to be very intuitive with what was happening and with the child spirit.

I held it tightly in my palm and contended to the great amount of sadness I felt in the object. The melancholy of the entity was felt down to the middle of my own animate spirit.

Then out of the blue, our cat started to meow loudly, as she turned her head like a computerized robot, following an invisible target. I stepped out of the bathroom and watched the small animal look toward the ceiling of the kitchen, with eyes dark and wide.

"What is it little kitty?" I asked the agitated pet.

She continued her motions, and then suddenly, arched her back, as her black tail fluffed three times its original size.

"Precious, it's all right! Calm down!" I asserted her.

The girls said nothing as they stared at the cat in a state of shock. Then unexpectedly and strangely enough, the feline stopped looking up and simply walked away and sat at her food bowl, and began to eat her breakfast.

At that instant, I concluded to call Father Stanley and ask him to come over and bless our home. I said out loud, "Don't worry, help is on its way."

After the girls were dropped off at school, and I arrived at my workplace, I immediately placed a call to St. Patrick's church. Coincidently, the church's cleric answered the phone. I was surprised to hear Father Stanley Nadolny's voice and instantaneously began to tell him what occurred earlier that morning.

I began with, "Good morning Father. This is Fran Maklary and I need your help."

"Yes, good morning to you as well, Fran. What is the matter?" answered the Father, and somehow knew instantly something was wrong and said, "Wait. You can't tell me over the phone can you?"

"I…"

"No, you can't. Do you want me to come to your house?" interrupted the priest.

"Yes. I need you to bless my home," I stated.

He retorted with, "Fine, fine. Let me see…Let me check my daily planner. I have a spaghetti dinner to attend this evening at 6:00. Can I come over before my appointment, around 5:45?"

"Yes. That'll be fine. Thank you Father."

I was a nervous wreck and thought about the girls being alone at the house, after school. I thought for a few minutes before calling my sister Sally. When I contacted her later that morning, I told her what happened, and asked if the girls could go over to her house after school. She generously agreed, and even thought about my dog Tootsie's well being, and picked her up and took her to her house as soon as she got off the phone with me. She couldn't take the cat with her because she's extremely allergic to all felines.

When I arrived home with the girls after work, we told my husband about the paranormal incident and informed him of the priest's scheduled arrival later that evening. Upon our entrance, Bill told us he had experienced something odd as well.

He said he was confused when he walked through the front door and realized the girls weren't home, but was immediately distracted from his thoughts to a disturbing sight. The two doll-like, angel ornaments on the Christmas tree were upside down and sitting on the center branches. As he showed us how they were placed, before he turned them right side up, Brittany interrupted his demonstration with a report of another incident, regarding another angel figure.

She said that a few days before, while doing her homework in her bedroom, a figurine mysteriously slid off the surface of her dresser, then levitated for one or two seconds, then fell to the floor!

After hearing that, Bill became instantly angry and said, "Come on little bastard, come and rock on the chair now!"

This entity was somehow causing a strange field of negative and frustrated emotions, making Bill and myself very protective over our children. This spirit was flashed to me as a young boy, from the age of five to maybe seven years of age. The boy has light brown hair, slender build, European descendant, and very hyperactive.

The hands of an adult male, maybe strangulation, was the cause of his death. His murder was long and dragged-out and filled with much pain and fear. The horrendous act occurred during the Christmas season of one of his saddest years of his short life. He had just experienced some sort of separation from his mother. She wasn't dead, just not with him.

His time of life is unclear, but is the very late 1800s or very early 1900s. The child-spirit is confused and has decided to cling to me. He identifies me as a mother and recognizes my maternal stature in the home.

Religion was a large part of his upbringing, until his mother left his side. The child, who calls himself John, does know who God is and says he remembers praying before meals, and at bedtime. He wants to remember Him. He needs to know how to get to Him, but the wall of dark and fog is too thick for him to see or feel anything. I was hoping with the help of the local cleric, we could try to push that obstacle out of the way, and finally clear the path for the lost soul's true designation.

After discussing the Christmas angels with my family, I changed into a pair of sweats and sweatshirt and went into the kitchen to make dinner. We didn't discuss what was going to happen later in the evening, and managed to enjoy a peaceful meal.

Time seemed too unusually swift by, making the arrival of the priest a nice surprise. The reverend entered the house with the normal greetings of handshakes and got right to the point of his visitation. He first asked us all what happened, listened, and preceded to recite from a small paperback book of ritual rites and prayers.

After reciting a prayer, he proceeded to sprinkle Holy Water, where we said we had experienced the most paranormal activity. He went to each bedroom, the bathroom, living area, kitchen, and even went outside in the back, where he stayed for quite a while, maybe feeling a strong sense of presence from the entity.

He prayed for the salvation of the lost soul and commanded it to abandon the house and to leave its residents alone. The priest was present for only a short time, and blessed us all with Holy Water and with his power of benedictions before he left for his special dinner.

"Good night and God Bless," said Father Nadonly, as he scurried out the door and headed toward his car, parked right outside.

I watched the priest's car lights turn on, then watch it drive away. That took me back to the moment of another cleric leaving my home, after another home blessing, of trying to rid other spirits from my place of childhood sanctuary. This reminiscent feeling verified my lifetime of emotional drains, with those who are drawn to my supernatural receptiveness, stubborn to stay with me, no matter where I live, no matter my age.

As anyone would expect, the entity seemed to disappear, leaving us to live in a respite state of comfort and giving us a chance to understand what had transpired. The spirit child seemed to appreciate an empty rocking chair, so I got rid of it. I made sure never to leave any chair resembling a rocking chair empty. I would leave a pillow in any wooden seat or always made sure a dining chair was pushed in all the way.

After the Christmas season passed, we didn't experience any more paranormal activity, but when Bill returned to the 'graveyard' shift, small things began to happen all over again. It seemed when he was present; the entity would retrieve and fade from our existence, hankering for maternal comfort, and for some reason, was afraid of the paternal.

On the day of my daughter Chelsie's first holy communion, I took several pictures of her in her white, floor-length gown. She had her long, light-brown hair up in curls, and along with the dress, wore the traditional white gloves and long veil, which is appropriate wear for the sacramental ceremony. The photos captured her innocence and happiness of the celebrated day, along with an unexpected shot of a supernatural capacity.

In one of the photos shot in the living room, two orbs were clearly seen. One was floating high above her head, and the other was hovering quite close to her side. I was very surprised to see two forms of floating energy in the pictures. Evidently, the child spirit was not alone, and most important, not gone.

Every few months, another incident involving eerie situations unfolded over the next year. The girls and I would hear footsteps near the bathroom when no one was in sight, and the children's bedroom television would turn on, without warning.

Brittany constantly complained about an invisible visitor pushing on her bed, sometimes hitting it hard, and resembling the sensation of a fist pounding the mattress in sequences of twos and threes.

During a very active night, both of the girls chose to sleep in my bed, since Bill was working the nightshift. I had a hard time going to sleep during that period of time myself and welcomed the company.

Right before I was going to get up for some water that same night, I heard voices in the living room. I thought I was dreaming, but then I heard a stranger's voice saying the name of my younger child. The voice sounded like a woman's. It was calling in a long, mellow-toned, whisper, "*Ch-el-s-ie…*"

The voice was at first distorted, and then I heard perfect pronunciation of the eerie voice clearly. A few seconds later, I could hear a low set of voices having some sort of conversation. I couldn't make out what they were actually saying, but nevertheless, I heard them. It was quite annoying.

Just when I thought I was losing my mind, Brittany, who was inches from my side, said, "Mom. Can you sleep with that noise? Do you hear them?"

"Yes…holy moly, I thought I was going crazy kid."

I looked over to her, barely seeing her figure in the dark. She grabbed her pillow and put it over her head and said, "Shut-up!"

"There you go Britt. Tell 'em."

"I just want to go to sleep."

"We said, SHUT-UP!" I shouted loudly. "That's enough!" As soon as I said that, they did.

This type of strange incident usually happened right around Christmas time, every year. During an evening of seasonal decorating, I was yet a victim to another phenomenon, at that house. For the first time in my life, I was physically attacked by an entity. Something I have never experienced before, and do not wish for it to happen again.

To add sparkle and cheer to our holiday season, Bill and I like to hang several strings of Christmas lights inside our home. As we worked as a well-practiced team of light hangers and enjoying holiday music, and our children sorting tree ornaments in the background, I felt the first small burning sensation of a scratch on my bare leg. (I loath to wear long pants, even during the winter, and choose to wear shorts most of the year.) I instinctively let go of the string of white lights I was holding and reached for the wound without saying a word. I shrugged of the pain, and continued to hold the lights while Bill continued to string them over the front doorway.

Minutes passed before I felt another singe of pain. Then another. They became more painful then before and forced me to stop what I was doing to see if I was bleeding.

At the sites of the pain, there were several red, long marks, resembling cat scratches. I automatically looked around to see if our pet cat was playing some kind of game with me. She is known to be mischievous from time to time.

Before I could saw a word, I felt another scratch on my right thigh. I looked down and saw one elongated, thin, cut begin to rapidly swell and itch.

"What the heck is that?" I finally said out loud.

Without stopping to look at me, Bill asked, "What's wrong!"

"Ouch! Waa…" I felt another shock of pain and saw another small lesion appear near the other one!

"Look Bill, something is scratching me!"

He looked down at me from atop the chair and said, "That's weird. Maybe you're scratching yourself, and don't know it."

I decided to stop helping with the light hanging, and asked the girls if they were ready to help with the tree ornaments. After we put the huge assortment of decorations in order, the three of us began to carefully place them on the artificial tree. It didn't take long for the eerie scratches to appear again, but this time on the other leg.

I went to the bathroom to inspect the abrasions. The new cuts were deeper set then the first. They also swelled faster and hurt more. I put peroxide on all of them, and mediated a message to the attacking entity. I called God's angels for protection against the assaulting banshee. I waited a few minutes before I returned to the living room and continued to pray for help.

When I did return, I could immediately feel the change of the mood in the room. By this time the girls were giggling and smiling and Bill was whistling to the melody of a Christmas song as he continued his work to illuminate the room with lights.

The following Christmas holiday, a new way of communication was tried by the child entity. He was coming to Brittany and I in our dreams. During the early month of December, I dreamt of an antique picture. It was of an unknown young boy, whom, by the look of the style of the picture, seemed to be around the turn-of-the-century. His picture was in an oval-shaped, dark and glossy frame, and the picture was turned yellow with age.

Even though the picture was obviously originally black and white, one could detect the colors of the subject. His hair light brown, and his hairstyle was of fashionable standards, the part was made in the middle and the length was past his ears. The boy was dressed in a white, buttoned-up, long-sleeved shirt with pearl buttons.

His facial expression seemed to be placid and his eyes seemed to gate his true depressed state of being. His face also appeared to be slightly chubby and his skin seemed porcelain.

I did not tell anyone about the dream, but coincidently Brittany told me about the similar nightmare she had a few nights later. She said the vision was of two people, a young boy and a tall man, with dark and layered hair. The two were intertwined in a destructive hold, as the man was strangling the child with his hands tightly wrapped around his neck.

In fast and violent shakes, the boy's head was jerked back and forth with the might of the dark man's grip, whose hair whipped around his head and neckline as he asphyxiated the child to death.

The child's entity was trying to tell why his life was cut short and was also relaying some of his torment to both of us. He tried over and over, to tell us his story. From the first time he learned how to collect the energy of our life-light and our inner-spirit, he has been attempting to free his soul from the earthbound prison he is in. In the dreams, he showed the face of his enemy, and his own innocent expression as well.

I have continuously prayed for the child-spirit's delivery to his true destiny, but just when I think he has left, peculiar things unravel around my house. For instance, while alone in the home during a spring morning, I was making my bed when suddenly; a comb flew out of the bathroom! With no one to blame, I turned toward the plastic comb on the floor, picked it up, and said to thin air, 'Cut it out, or I'm going to spank you!"

I have come to the conclusion that the child-entity likes to be talked too in a maternal tone and manner, and will typically quiet down, after it is spoken to in just that way. Providing more evidence that he is a child.

Chapter XIV

Three decades have passed since I witnessed paranormal activity tracing back to a man named Hans and a woman named Annabelle. Over the years I have often thought of the sad spirits, wondering if they finally found peace. Did they ever reunite with their families and friends in the afterlife and finally find their way back to God?

Just the thought of the couple living in a comatose state as floating souls in a living world, is unbearable for anyone to muster. I constantly prayed for the entities' liberation from their earthly ties and to their heavenly glory over my lifetime. The obsession tried true in my subconscious as well.

After we moved from the home, I had a recurring dream for several years. Between the ages of ten and fourteen, I dreamed I was levitating in the living room and outside in the driveway, floating then without warning, falling gently to the floor. I was always alone in my dreams, but the feeling that someone was standing behind me was a constant.

At the time I didn't recognize the dream as a call for help from the entities, but now as a matured psychic, I understand the magnetic pull.

It was the morning of my 34th birthday and the first thing that ran through my mind, oddly enough, was Annabelle and Hans. Why were they calling to me? What did they want? Why now, after all these years? Did my birthday play and important roll in the reception of the messages calling from the other side? Whatever the reason, the spirits were definitely trying to contact me.

After my girls left for school, I poured myself a second mug of coffee and began to wonder what I was going to do, since my husband was working the morning shift, and I was going to be alone until early afternoon.

Memories of my childhood began to fill my mind as I sipped the steaming hot liquid and gazed at the scenery through my large living room window. The breeze shook the leaves from the Arizona Oaks in the park-like yard, and through the glass pane, I could hear the birds singing. The scene brought me back to the time of my purest innocence and probably the time when I was most open to unearthly presences, the time of my early childhood.

Thoughts of returning to that spot began to fill my head as well as questions regarding the traumatic experiences. Were the banshees free from their earthly bondage? Was poor Annabelle still restrained by Hans? Did the exorcism work?

"Well, there's only one way to find out. Go and see for yourself," I said out loud.

As I showered, I began to think about the images of Annabelle. I thought about the clothes she was wearing when I saw her as a small child. The faded lace blouse and an ankle length skirt that hung on her thin, frail, body. The gentleness she generated as she stared at me while I was in bed. That poor, poor woman, was she finally at rest? My eyes began to fill with tears. Those recollections of Annabelle were surprisingly dear to me.

As I dressed in a pair of shorts, tank top, and a denim jacket, I remembered my camera.

"Let's see if I can catch those suckers on film," I whispered.

At the time I was living very close to the actual site and decided to walk instead of drive. As I traveled down Tombstone Canyon, my stomach began to tighten, my hands began to clam, and my heart began to race.

"This is as exciting as hell. Let's see what happens."

Before I knew it, I was at the base of the plateau that led straight up to the house.

"Funny, this slope seems a lot steeper than I remember," I said in between a couple of heavy breaths.

I could barely see the staircase leading to the entrance of the front yard due to the glare of the sun pounding on the road. My apprehension was rapidly turning into trepidation. For the sake of the occupant, I didn't want to stir up trouble by 'hunting' for something that might now be nonexistent.

As I stood in front of the house, I asked God to cover me with his blood and to send his angels for protection. I took a deep breath, crossed myself, and began to climb the cement stairs. As I scaled the steps, I looked down to where I had drawn scenes from life in chalk, ranging from purple suns to red skies. Sweet, yet passionate pictures created by a young girl, during a time that was also filled with the same kind of strange energy.

The memories became more and more clear, as I got closer to the house. The memories began to run through my mind like a slide show. Frame by frame, my childhood flashed back with intense reality. I had finally returned to the spot where it all began for me, and where it ended for *them.*

When I arrived at the top, I stopped and stood behind a black iron gate. I scanned the house and was surprised to see it painted with the same old brown and adobe colors. (It always looked brown and orange to me, but my father insisted it was Adobe, and not orange). The windows were bare and boxes of different spray paint cans were spread all over the floor of the wooden porch. The house seemed to be in poor shape, but by the looks of it, it was going through some sort of renovation.

As I continued to stand in front of the locked gate, I gazed over to my right. My beautiful playground, it was falling apart. The yard seemed unattended and abandoned. As I stared at the empty, dirt-filled yard, I could almost hear my own child's voice laughing as I swung on my colorfully decorated swing set. I could hear my mother's Mexican music blaring from the living room and the rest of the family laughing and carrying on in the back yard, as well.

The leaves of the two large cottonwood trees lined in front of the house began to shake in an unexpected burst of warm air. The natural occurrence pulled me back to reality. After taking a deep breath, I looked over to the other side of the front yard and spotted my most favorite tree in the entire yard, now nearing its death.

The tree's roots were exposed and the hill it was resting on, was almost gone. I flashed back to my childhood again, reminiscing about the summers playing under the same oak tree. I was enjoying myself as I recalled the special serenity and happiness I felt in that particular area, remembering it as if it was yesterday.

Below that spot, a garden of tomatoes, carrots, and green chilies, and a variety of other vegetables grew, but now in its place, a half torn down gazebo stood.

I remember that garden and how my mother planted the vegetables during the spring when she was in her early thirties and when I was too young for school. We had many free afternoons full of digging and watering seedlings, and a lot of time alone, but together.

Giggles would fill the spring air as my mother and I happily worked in our garden. She would carry on about the yummy salads and hot salsa she was going to make, when the vegetable patch was completed.

A distant dog's bark broke me from another trance and made me jump and grab on to the side rail of the iron fence. I then decided to turn around and walk down the hill toward School House Inn Bed & Breakfast, a business located down the hill and directly across the street from where I was standing.

As I walked around the B & B building, I saw an older gentleman working on an antique car. I headed toward him and waited for him to turn around, thinking he could hear my footsteps on the graveled driveway. He never turned his head in acknowledgment.

"Excuse me sir, may I interrupt you for a minute," I asked.

The man replied, without turning and continuing with his work from the open hood of the car said, "Sure." The man was tall, thin, and wearing a large brimmed, felt hat, with hands covered in grease.

"I was wondering if you knew who owns the house behind this building?" Before he could answer, I added, "Is this your bed and breakfast?"

The elderly man put his wrench down on a rag placed on the fender of the classic car, rose to a straight standing position and said, "Yes, this is my business."

"Well, I used to live in that house as a child, and interesting events occurred there. I am in the process of writing a book about those unexplained experiences. Does anyone live there?"

"Yeah, he lives there and is renovating it during his spare time," said the business owner.

"I wasn't sure if anyone did. I didn't want to enter the premises without permission."

He nodded in agreement.

I began to feel a little silly telling a complete stranger about my quest into the supernatural. I continued with my questioning.

"Um. I was hoping you did know the owner because I wanted to take pictures of the house. Do you think he would mind?"

"If that's all you want to do, are take pictures of the outside, then I don't think he would mind. Just don't get stuck while you're walking around."

"I know what you mean. I saw a lot of weak places where the yard is caving in. The front porch has boards holding its right retaining wall. I'll be careful. Thank you," I said while extending my hand for a handshake. "Thanks for your friendliness and help."

"Sure. See you around," he replied.

As I walked back toward the road, I heard the man's wrench cranking back to work. The sun was higher in the sky, the morning was gaining temperature, and so was I.

As I returned to the house, I decided to start up the incredibly steep driveway positioned directly to the right side of the antique looking house. Again, the past flashed back in my mind. I remembered my father working meticulously every day, building a respectable driveway, up that extremely vertical hill. I recalled him stirring a brand of ready-mix cement little by little, as he climbed the mountain with concrete strips for each side of the car's wheels. Now, a new, solid and a smooth cement driveway take its place.

I quickly found myself at the top of the mountain and felt my heart pounding hard. I couldn't tell if was from the climb or my nerves.

As I stood in the old parking area, I thought to myself, "Man, I forgot the highway was this close to the house."

The roadway is approximately fifty-feet from the backdoor. I remembered after a few seconds, how often the sounds of the passing semi-trucks would send me off to sleep, late at night.

I stared at the huge, deep, ditch on the right side of the parking area and driveway, which used to be off-limits to my siblings and me. I turned to the site of the place where the dogs' pen used to be. It looked the same, minus the fencing and pets, of course.

It dawned on me that I had my camera. As I took it out of my bag, I studied the back of the house, where the laundry entrance used to be. I took the lens cap off the camera, turned it on, and noticed the new owner had all of his gardening tools hanging along the wall. Exposed boards made it look of 1880s fashion. It looked neat, but dangerously close to the time of early Bisbee.

"*Click*," went my first shot.

I was incredibly calm, considering the circumstances. I turned to face the side yard where the crab apple tree was. The apples of that fruit tree were so sour and so green…

"Wait, where is it?" I said in astonishment.

The tree used to sit smack in the middle of that great big side yard, but now it was gone. I took pictures of the area filled with boards and other building material, which has now, took the place of the hickory.

"*Click*."

The sound of the camera seemed amplified due to the severe quiet. A very eerie feeling began to come over me. As I tried to ignore those unusual vibes, I decided the angles I was shooting from were not what I wanted, and headed for the set of stairs that my father had also constructed. Then I focused my eyes on the steps leading down from the backyard level to where the entrance to the basement was located. My memories of that particular area of the house were filled with severe coldness, dread, and a place that seemed to spawn the feelings of death.

As I climbed down the steps positioned beneath one of the dining room windows, I heard footsteps coming from inside the home.

I froze and took in a huge, deep breath and turned my head around to look inside and saw no one.

"Hello. Is anyone there?" I shouted.

No reply.

"Come on Fran, get a grip," I whispered to myself while shaking my head.

I returned my attention to the basement door and continued down the rest of the cement steps. As I finally arrived in front of the basement, I stared down toward the entrance and became very uneasy.

"*Click.*"

The entrance was surrounded with overgrown ivy vines and leaves. The steps that led down to the wooden door were exactly as I remembered. They were covered in powdery dirt, unevenly paved and still as ugly as hell.

I took several pictures of the entrance, and when I looked at the digital counter on the camera, I felt that amazing familiarization of the presence of an irritated banshee. The same terrifying feelings that could only be tied to the same old entities, had very abruptly, smothered me with their supernatural suffrages. I could feel *them* looking at me through the windows above me and without hesitation I said very loudly, "My God, *they're still here.* Please God, cover me with your blood, and protect me from their grips."

Despite my tremendous horror, I chose to continue shooting pictures and focused the camera on the door, suspiciously now opened half way.

"Whoa, wait a minute. That door was closed."

I trembled as I spoke in a low voice. "This is quickly turning wicked."

I stood ice-covered with fear and too petrified to move. The energy from the two entities quickly draped me in dead coldness. The morbid and depressed emotions from the dead were swarming around me. Swirling into a thick cloud of pure terror.

I gathered enough strength to look up at the window positioned above the basement door. With heart pounding and palms hot with sweat, I saw a dark shadow, shaped in the figure of a man. His silhouette slowly turned into a foggy vision; just clear enough to make his structure detectible.

Still glued in the same spot, and too afraid to move, I knew I had to leave. I was definitely unwelcome and my well-being was dangerously unsecured. I maintained my aim toward the house, as I mechanically turned my head toward my right and felt the angry presence on my other side. His demure was filled with enough aggression to intimidate my usual confidence of confronting such negative energy, and made me feel extremely endangered.

I quickly flipped my head back toward the house and closed my eyes. His energy was gaining momentum, as well as my own blood pressure. My body was in position to head up the stairs and sprint to my freedom, but when I took my first step to do so, I felt an incredible amount of magnetic pull behind me, and felt a heavy hand push me forward!

My heart was in my throat and I can't remember getting from the spot in front of the basement entrance, or how I got up the side stairs and to the parking area, but I do recall being pushed from behind.

An infuriated force pressed me forward as I felt the sunlight dimming around me, as I was completely horror-struck and felt as if I didn't leave at that exact moment, I would be trapped there forever.

As I found myself at the top of the driveway, I realized what I was doing. *This lost soul can't hurt me. I am alive and full of God.*

I turned completely around and screamed, "I cast you out in the name of God!" I pulled up the strap of my camera bag that was falling off my shoulder and continued, "Begone, evil spirit, begone!"

Still petrified, but now with a better grip on what was happening, I turned toward the house and took more pictures.

"Click. Click."

Regardless of being in a dazed state, I made it down the driveway and walked with a slow pace. As I made it closer to the street I heard banging and yelling from the yard, now above me. Eerie voices rang in my ears and a woman's cry was moaning from the front yard and back around. Her murmuring cries were filled with spine-chilling sobs that seemed to echo throughout the canyon.

Her wailings were followed by a bellowing male voice. The strong and menacing timbre scared me into a quicker pace. I scurried down the last few steps of the driveway, and then made a right, straight up the hill and back to my original starting point. I was in front of the main entrance of the house within seconds of the last pictures snapped, and strangely, now very angry.

"I'm right here you asshole! I'm not a kid anymore! You can't and will not hurt me...!" I was losing control and had to regain composure.

I stood at the bottom of the front steps, then took a deep breathe and chose to walk further up the steep road. I turned my entire body toward the house near the empty lot adjacent to the structure's left, and bowed my head. I had to bring myself to a meditative state of spiritual strength in order to protect my own soul from the corrupted entity still trapped there.

After a few moments passed, I finally regained my normal rhythm of breathing. *They're still here Damn it, they are still here.* I just couldn't believe it.

As I regained some level-headedness, I stared at the house, feeling the spirits' presence. They were now quiet, but the energy of the dead couple was still perceptible.

"Why are you still here? What's the matter with you?" I asked.

Becoming fearless, I walked back down the hill and up to the locked gate and stood there like a valiant combatant, waiting for some sort of retort, but none came.

"Don't you understand you're dead? You have passed on! Aren't you tired of this place? Go home..." A long silence followed my outburst. I took another deep breath and crossed myself and began to say *The Lord's Prayer.*

"Our Father who art in heaven,..."

The cold air began to melt into the warm sunlight as I serenaded the prayer.

"...give us our daily bread..."

As I finished the last word out loud, so did the supernatural calamity. I began to take pictures of the front windows and before I could take another photo, I saw a shadow move behind the living room window.

"Click."

Then I aimed the camera toward the other window, which used to be my parent's bedroom.

"Click."

The sad outcome of my small journey back to my beginnings explained the strange messages I received from the entities. Their sad and poignant saga continues, despite the prayers of many. This purely depressed scene proves that only a soul can save itself from damnation. Only self can save self.

My intentions upon returning were not to find Hans and Annabelle, but not to find them. I really did hope they were gone. How many years will they stay on that site? I don't know, but they must realize they are in control and must find solution to their freedom by releasing all earthly ties of guilt, anger, and despair. They must free themselves from their own imprisonment by accepting they have passed and must travel to the other side.

Our house still stands, as it goes through another state of renovation, and home to another personage. The long-ago, lived couple, still continuing as paired entities in the antediluvian home, remaining even after an exorcism and several blessings, from several generations of God loving people.

Amazingly, after all this time, another person, whom I didn't know had experienced 'disturbances' in the same place, a few years later then me. The individual is my younger brother, Albert.

He was born approximately two years after the height of the haunting and lived there until he was three years old. During a conversation regarding various paranormal experiences, I had discovered that he remembered certain details experienced at the Tombstone Canyon house, concluding that my own psychic visions were registering true.

Many of our family members claim to have an incredible ability of remembering far back into our childhood, as early as two years of age. I personally remember sitting in the highchair, (surely before reaching the age of three) feeling a warm and wet, cloth rubbing the food excess off my cheeks. I remember smelling the different scents of food on the stove and the wire curlers adoring my mother's head. A memory clear as present day and lived out decades ago.

With that in mind, here are the recollections of a three-year-old:

Albert said he remembers playing with a large, rubber ball in the hallway leading to our parent's bedroom and the attic, and to one of the entrances of the bathroom. He stated he was sitting on the floor, directly in front of the doorway of the master bedroom, throwing the ball against the nearest wall. As he continued his repetitive motion, the ball accidentally hit the corner of the open bathroom door and rolled into the unoccupied bedroom.

Before the curlyhead toddler could get his little body up to retrieve the toy, it mysteriously rolled back into the hall and toward his direction. The toddler accepted the toy and innocently enough, continued to play.

The ball, after many throws, eventually went off-target once more, and ended back in the bedroom. This time the ball was not peacefully returned. Right in front of the tot's eyes, the ball was jerked up to midair, thrown violently across our parent's bedroom, and bounced from wall to floor, to wall, and back to the ground!

Albert said before he could let out a fright-filled scream, he saw a dark, gray shadow whiz right by him, with great powered speed. Along with it, passed a sudden cold burst of air. He then reported to recall one of our eldest sisters running to him and jerking him into her arms. (During those years, the twins looked so much alike, it was hard to distinguish their difference.)

During the same time-period, my brother mentioned two other incidents, which brought shivers to his spine and mine, as he described them.

I never personally felt the front porch of the house we are speaking of, to have entity energies, but Albert did. He said he could remember playing alone on the large porch with his collection of little cars. While enjoying himself, he recalled hearing a murmuring sound resembling the voices of two people, a man and a woman. He said the voices seemed to sound as if they were trying to argue quietly, at first, and then they accelerated to full-out screaming!

Apparently, he was too young to explain his experiences to our mother, and any other family members.

"I really don't recall telling anyone about the incidents," he stated.

He reported to have heard the same eerie voices again, this time, during a visit from our sister Stella's boyfriend, and in the same area of the porch. He said they were positioned on the bottom porch steps and played catch with a small ball. The trio continuously threw the ball back and forth for a good while, until a throw was projected off-target. Albert raced to retrieve the ball that had bounced up to the floor of the porch and unexpectedly, heard the same strange voices. The murmurs were faint, but still apparent and arguing. He ignored the frightening pitches, and said he returned to the attention of the teenaged couple.

Those altercations resemble my own, as a very young child in that same house. The supernatural scenes were at first, filled with a peaceful flow of energy, than without warning, a dark and raging one took its place.

Did Annabelle feel attracted to the baby boy as she did to me? Was she trying to find solace in the presence of children? Did poor Annabelle try to find a child of her own to escape the guilt of losing her own and the dark energy binding her?

My brother also recalled our mother telling him about a time when she and our sister Sally were outside taking photos of him, while he was still small enough for a baby walker.

It was during a nice, spring day, and an afternoon of enjoying the nice climate of Bisbee. My mother let Albert play in the thin grass of the front yard in his walker, while she and Sally talked. Without notice, Albert began to giggle, and then laugh almost uncontrollably, for no apparent reason.

The laughing child urged mom to direct Sally to go inside and retrieve the camera, to capture his amusing chuckles. Albert said he was told that mom was very confused to the reason for his actions, since no one was near or playing with him.

During and after the time the pictures were taken, the baby continued to laugh and ignore his mother. Finally, mom grabbed him from his seat, and hugged and kissed her babe, calming his mysterious laughter.

In the actual pictures, you can see the baby with a wide grin, and laughing as if circus clowns were entertaining him. Albert conveyed his thoughts about the matter, thinking possibly the reason he was forced into billows of laughter, was because he saw *Annabelle*?

After my brother finished telling me about his own experiences and connections with the entities, my own interpretation of the couple seemed to play out in perfect sequenced chapters of time.

The murmured voices my brother heard, was the never-ending conflict of good and evil. Annabelle's gesture of gentleness of rolling the ball back to the toddler, was quickly interrupted by Hans throwing it in a violent rage, was his constant need to punish his wife for the death of their own babies. The action also proved his powerful hold over her. Hans was, and still is in the dimension between heaven and earth, and acts as a controlling and powerful unit to his demented selfish plan of staying earthbound.

His blame for the death of his children caused him to finally lose his mind. His murderess' actions were forced by years of painful experiences he had endured as a living soul, were shortly relieved by the birth of his own daughter. The short life of the child was the only real person who loved Hans unconditionally, and without any criticism.

This poor soul, how will he ever escape himself? Will he ever release Annabelle and pass over to the other side as well? Annabelle can break the chains of fear and guilt that is keeping her from the reunion with her precious baby and other family members. She is the only one that can call to heaven and ask to see the glow of the glorious entrance of everlasting life. It is only she that can walk herself to the 'other side.'

The same goes for Hans, but he must be aware of his own sins and ask God for forgiveness, and finally find his own way home. That will be a happy reunion of family and friends, for the depressed couple from the 1800s, if only they would realize how easily their suffering could end, just by accepting their time on earth has expired.

Nevertheless, the entities' heartrending story continues, such as the century-old house still stands in historic Bisbee, Arizona. The three are unscathed by the changes of time and seemingly undying in two different realms of perpetuity.

Chapter XV

One of the most favorite places for me to find peace is in the mountains. Such as the puma thrives, and lies on a grass-covered rock, I too feel full and rested. The high altitude and almost always-beautiful views seen from a mountaintop are for me, one of Mother Earth's sweetest gifts to the human spirit.

The even flow of sudden bursts of clean and aromatic air; can cleanse the mind of negative thoughts and rejuvenate the soul with hope and prayer. The earthly energy found on untamed peaks are powerful healing forces, which push the wind under the wings of the wild hawk and eagle, propelling them higher and higher.

My entire life has been mostly lived in the mountains of Bisbee and surrounding towns. Evolving my spirituality with higher degrees of nature's positive energies, and surrounding my hopes and dreams with great aspirations for future generations of a thriving and prosperous people.

All the things I have experienced in life, from being one of the last generations of a 'Canyon Rat,' (an adoring nickname for children reared on Tombstone Canyon) a child of generations of Bisbee miners, and a production of being fostered in a community of where my family roots run deep, I have endured the raptures of learning how to cope with my supernatural sensitivity under a blanket of blessed comfort.

Home has been the backbone of my increased development of my ability to communicate with people who have died, and refused upon the grace of free will, to continue on, toward eternal rest. The restless spirits of Bisbee have generated the spark of my psychic vision for their existence in various sites in surrounding areas, pulling me closer for the transmission of their messages. They demand my complete attention and add confusion to the reason why they refuse to leave, staying as an earthbound soul and unwilling to hear about eternal freedom.

I at times do not want to hear the eerie knocks at the doors, the taps and invisible footsteps, that surround my body, but I must continue to listen for the simple cries of the souls who have lost their way. This is my calling from our Higher Power, to help them cross over.

There are no impossible aspirations for the living, or for the dead. It is not a maddening idea to believe that the possibilities of suffrage in the afterlife can be avoided and stripped completely from the tortured and trapped spirit in a confused state of purgatory, with the help of prayer.

Taken from the True Catholic Website: *As nothing defiled can enter Heaven (Rev. 21-27), there must necessarily exist a state of cleansing or purgation usually called "purgatory."*

Along with the flashes of violent deaths, and emotional pain, displayed for me by the various beings of the supernatural realm, I was also given an insight to the pain they commence upon unsuspecting victims, who currently reside in their haunted lands or structures. The haunting spirits of any site, in any town in the world, know nothing of the fear and disturbing feelings they generate to unsuspecting individuals.

The unrested dead do not know of the terror and mayhem caused by their egocentric decision of clinging to planet earth. The painstaking process of distinguishing what is real and what is not, can punish the mental well-being of an otherwise healthy individual.

All of God's people have the ability to feel the energies of those who have walked the ground before them, but those willing to respond to the unexplainable force of the paranormal, will empower his gift of eternal peace, by helping them find it.

I am a simple person who is making her way through life, hoping for the best, while trying to stay focused on the future. I try to stay away from those individuals who are negative and thrive on gossip and ill-willed feelings. These types of people are not healthy for the spirit and mind.

God wants his children to stay focused and uncontrolled by such corruption, which is sadly, very much a part of life in any given society. If we can keep our concentration on the positive side of life, then we can continue our preservation as a Christian populace.

This theory of keeping negative energies to a slim minimum can press the animus spirits to become weak and powerless. If we can keep our own integrity strong as we live each day, the time of death will be much more clear, and the light of God better focused. When our spirit is cleared of vindictive people, our soul will have more room for the holy spirit of God, making the rest easy to claim.

I have learned through life-experiences, life is good, but when we make terrible choices and are fogged with self-righteous motivations, the inner-spirit can become confused to the real mission of existence, and become lost. If we can keep a clear-mind attempt toward the achievements geared toward moral direction, then when our time is over here on earth, the transformation from body to spirit will be easy. We will not end-up like the confused banshees that walk on old, worn, creaking floors of their self-imprisoned places of earthbound Bondage. Do we not suffer enough while we are alive, creeping through a lifetime of mistakes and bad choices?

The lost souls, which have penetrated my own sensory, are individuals who did not think before turning their back from the completion for their livelong mission. I can almost understand the children who are empowered by a grip of mysterious reasoning to 'stay put,' due to their lack of mature knowledge of what is on the other side of the shadow of death. Maybe, the dark before the light is what is torturing their innocent spirits, clouding the beam of glorious radiance, which would bridge their soul to peaceful immortality.

But what about those of mature status, and why do they become disoriented during the time of death? A spirit that is attached to an adult body, of experienced mind and faith surely must feel the impact of livelong lessons of good and evil.

But what about those who choose to take their own lives, and how they become the most tormented spirits of all. Suffering, as much or more than they did when they were alive. At the moment of their self-inflicted death, they must feel the enraging heat from the threshold transcending it to a hellish place of a worse affliction then before.

Taken from the True Catholic Website: *The fire will assay the quality of everyone's work; if his work abides which he has built thereon, he will receive reward: if his work burns he will lose his reward, but himself will be saved, yet so as through fire. (I Corinthians 3:13-15)*

Those are punished in hell who die in mortal sin; they are deprived of the vision of God and suffer dreadful torments, especially that of fire, for all eternity.

-The he will say to those on his left hand, "Depart from me, accursed ones, into the everlasting fire which was prepared for the devil and his angels." (Matthew 24:41)

If the soul of a suicide death actually passes through the entry of perdition, it must feel the scalding pain of such a moral sin, and the guilt of doing so. These are the souls who do know they have left this life, and in their infuriating madness, refuse with that same awareness to 'stay put'.

They may walk this earth with the same emotional deranged thoughts, or convey to the state of 'feeling sorry' for themselves and hoping to communicate with those they left behind, driving them further into madness. When I come upon that type of selfish powered entity, filled with questionable capabilities, I call to the peaceful energies of heaven and Mother Earth.

Taking the memory of such places as the mountain peaks and the power of prayer, urges the forces of moral standards, to devour the derogatory vibes of the disturbed spirit. This meditation will drive it toward the ageless amity of God, or push it away from me, and protect my spiritual health.

Even though I have lived most of my life with a diversity of unearthly presences, I do from time to time, become very afraid. I don't care what any other self-proclaimed mediums say regarding the sometimes-horrible visions set before them, and how it doesn't petrify them down to the bare bone. If a person claims to have an extrasensory power and says what they 'see' doesn't bother them, then they are either liars or not true psychics.

Sometimes I really dislike the things I can feel. It is hard to cope with at times, but I have no way to block those energies, I have been open to them too long. Maybe it's not that, it might actually be that I don't want to hinder the insights of another realm, and I can't imagine not being able to sense energies of paranormal nature.

Despite my trepidation from time to time, I am almost always eager to investigate unusual disturbances. Whether it is an inexplicable disruption from an active poltergeist within my own domain, or if it is an entity that is disturbing another, I want to find out 'whom' it is, and why 'he' or 'she' is earthbound.

I want to know what caused the death of the person with such ambition or great ignorance to keep their soul in the place they adored as a living person, or just can't grasp the idea they have died. I want to help that spirit understand what has happened to them, and make them realize they can leave this place for another, where guilt, pain, and terror do not exist. A state of being that is filled with a measure of peacefulness not imaginable to any soul, living or departed.

It is a dissipation of time, to walk this earth in a hypnotic state, dumbfounded and lonely, believing that you are living, keeping yourself in a state of disbelief. But, that is what a lost soul is doing, wasting time that could be spent in perpetual bliss, with family members who have also died and are waiting for the soul of a loved one to join them.

When my 'time' finally does come, I know my deceased's family members will greet me. My mother, she will be the first being I see; my maternal grandfather, he will come with her. Even though I never met him, he knows me well and has as come to me in spirit, many times.

Very often I have the urge to visit his grave, and many times, I have felt his presence. His demeanor is different from all others, who have come to me, in one way or another. He died in the late 1930s and has been in the state of 'Glory' for a long time. He doesn't come to me in my dreams, nor does he show up in the middle of the night, standing at the end of my bed, but transmits in as a very strong support system.

At certain times in my life, my grandfather, has been at my side, giving me strength and determination from the 'other side.' I can actually feel the love and admiration he has for me. I have a small, wallet-size, picture of him in a clear frame set out on a shelf in the living room. He wanted to be 'out', so he could watch over my small family. I'm sure he will be with my mother when they meet me at heaven's gate.

For now, while I walk this earth I will enjoy life with a strong and clear mind and soul. I feel death around me on a day-to-day basis, but carry the light of God's great gift, the Holy Spirit. This is the fire and strength that keep me going from beginning to end. It empowers my soul for the journey and my mission in life.

My paranormal experiences have all been different and with individual moral lessons. They tell the stories of everyday people, how they died, and what mistakes may have been made, trapping them in a frightening and lonely domain of earthbound hell.

I have been placed on this world with the same free will everyone has, but hope to use it with respect and intelligence, and as an unstoppable instrument during my lifetime. I just want to live this time on earth as a modest soul, ready to fend off self-indulgent personalities who walk with heavy hearts and unclear minds. I want to stay away from the sort of people who are controlled by political debauchery, ready to do anything to make a place for themselves in their circle of insecure and back stabbing societies.

I want to worship God without the attention of an audience of churchgoers only interested in seeing who and how often they are attending the house of the Lord. The members of this assemblage are 'Religious People.' They read God's Word, but do not live by it. Their positions and possessions hold them down, and keep them from a deep relationship with God.

To have the complete freedom of talking to the pure power of creation, all day and every day, is one of the sweetest and most endearing forms of worship a soul can demonstrate. Keeping the spirit focused on His preordained mission is another pure form of loving and respecting our Higher Power's wishes for the souls of this world.

Remember to allow a time of remembrance for those who have left this place we call life, and donate a few seconds of your day to prayer for the living and the dead. In any city, town, or rural area, someone has come before you. Do not forget them, for they may roam this earth in a sad state of spiritual bondage, or exist freely as a dear memory, now living in glorious place.

Taken from the True Catholic Website: Purgatory: The King James Bible teaches (a) that some sins are forgiven in the next world; (b) that some souls are saved in the next word "by fire"; and that it is useful and beneficial to pray for the dead. 2 Macahabees, 12-46: (This is one of the Old Testament books omitted from the Protestant Bible). It is therefore a holy and wholesome thought to pray for the dead and that they may be loosed from their sins.

History is a very important part of your life, whether it is your family's or it is of an entire population. Those who lived before want to leave a legacy filled with hard-learned lessons, so you can avoid the same suffering they had once endured.

The young pioneer; the spiritual Native American; the prideful Mexicans; and all other world citizens have made it through the pressed soils of life's ground, as they strolled and sometimes stumbled through their time on Earth. They have left timeless records of lifetime experiences, priceless memories, and divine hope for each future generation as each century passed.

If we can take notes from 'history's' lesson book, and involve them in everyday life, then our time on earth can be lived more suitable and less ignorant. Making this place an easier one to leave when it is time.

Forgiveness is another essential virtue to have in order to completely pass over to the other side. This is a hard merit to acquire if one is a victim of emotional abuse or physical horror. We must all learn to forgive our enemies and bless those who wish us harm.

If we have no animosity left in our hearts at the time of death, then we have one reason less to want to stay earthbound. If we can manage to reconcile with those '*who trespass against us*,' then we can ascend to Our Father with great lightness and with great pride.

I hope that the message I have so carefully tried to convey, has been recited correctly and without corruption. I have taken this assignment with great pride and hope I was successful to discourse the empowerment of life and what can happen during the time we make passage to death.

Thank you, my two grandfathers. Thank you, mother. Thanks to all creation. Their life goes on and on. Though they are far, they are always near, hearing all voices that call their names in the light that has been given through the glory of God, shining through the dark of death and into the world of brilliance.

Our journey on this planet will end, and when that time comes forth, do not be afraid, but rejoice in the gift of everlasting life. Be ready to take what has been promised to you and reveal in the light. Do not turn around and return to the bitter air of the dusty walls of the place you once inhabited, but go ahead into the light, and become eternally free. Let the Angels surround you and hear their harmonious voices sing with rejuvenations of your final journey to your place of grandeur, and for your happy return home…at last.

Printed in the United States
17763LVS00001B/370